"There are a lot of beautiful things in this world."

Something about the slow, solemn way Garret said that made her stop turning, a shiver going over her. He was watching her, hands planted low on his hips, his bad one seeming to perch comfortably for once. His shoes were now on the ground beside him. "Addy…"

"Yes?" Her breath caught in her throat.

He took a step closer. "I think I'm about to do something incredibly stupid."

"I doubt that." And if the look on his face was any indication, she was in complete agreement.

"Just how drunk are you?"

"Am I acting like I am? I didn't even drink the whole beer. I'm just so glad to be out here tonight…" She hesitated, then decided to just say it. "With you."

"I was hoping you'd say that."

In a second, he had closed the gap between them, his right hand encircling her wrist and tugging her to him.

And when his head came down, she knew the kiss was coming. Only this time, it would be different than the previous one. Very, very different.

Dear Reader,

Twists. Life can sure throw them at us, can't it? Sometimes those twists bring great things, and sometimes they bring pain and confusion. Neurosurgeon Garret Stapleton learns all about those twists when tragedy steals everything he once held dear, including his career. But life keeps on turning, and those twists keep coming, and soon he is brought face-to-face with the very thing he fears the most. Garret has to decide whether to rise to the challenge…or run.

Thank you for joining Garret and ER doctor Adelina Santini as they navigate the treacherous waters of heartache and loss. And maybe, just maybe, they can overcome the past and learn to love again.

I hope you enjoy reading about this very special couple as much as I've loved writing their story!

Love,

Tina Beckett

ONE NIGHT TO CHANGE THEIR LIVES

———

TINA BECKETT

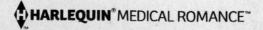

Recycling programs
for this product may
not exist in your area.

ISBN-13: 978-1-335-64141-0

One Night to Change Their Lives

First North American Publication 2019

Copyright © 2019 by Tina Beckett

Printed in U.S.A.

To my family: here's to twists.

CHAPTER ONE

PEARLS WERE NOT her thing. Not anymore.

Adelina Santini dropped the necklace into its velvet lined jeweler's box, snapped the lid shut and put it in the growing stack of things to donate to the hospital's charity auction. Five years of marriage and the necklace and her wounded pride were the only things she had to show for it.

The bed had been stripped of sheets, pillows and the comforter—she'd jammed everything into the trash along with her wedding pictures. But even with brand-new bedclothes, she couldn't face sleeping in that room. So she'd spent the last six weeks sleeping on the couch, and that was where she'd stay until she could decide what to do about the bed, about the house…about everything. Divorce papers were filed and her soon-to-be ex had moved in with the woman she'd caught him cheating with—the same day she'd walked in on them. Getting rid of those pearls—his wedding gift to her—was the first step toward leaving an ugly part of her past behind. At least she hoped so.

All she wanted was to wash her hands of him and never see him again. But he was an EMT who regularly brought patients to her hospital. Unless she moved to another city, she would see him. Daily at times. So far, those encounters had been far from fun. There was no way she was going to let her distaste at seeing him drive her out of her job, though.

Abandoning her task for the hundredth time that week, she went to shower and get dressed for work. Right now, her job was her only salvation. The fact that she arrived before her shift started and left long after it was over was no one's business but her own. With that thought, she stepped under the stinging flow of hot water and waited for it to wash away all her troubles.

A half hour later, juggling five boxes of items for the auction, she walked through the doors of the emergency room of Miami's Grace Hospital and headed for the staff lounge to drop off what she'd brought. Five feet from the door, a familiar voice stopped her in her tracks.

"Dr. Santini, could I see you in my office for a minute?"

Peering over the stack, her eyes widened as she saw she was right. Garret Stapleton, the hospital administrator, stood with one shoulder propped against a nearby wall, arms crossed over his chest. A hint of biceps made a rare flush of warmth go through her.

Lord, Addy, what is wrong with you?

Then he moved toward her, and she took a quick step back, the parcels teetering for a second. The heat in her face turned red hot.

"Let me help you with those."

"It's okay. I've got them. Just a few things for the auction."

Why did he want to talk to her? Had she done something wrong? She'd been at this hospital for several years—longer than he had, in fact. And ever since her husband had walked out, her view of the world had shifted, opened up. That view now encompassed the sexy administrator in a way that made her cringe.

In her growing panic, the boxes tilted sideways, the jeweler's container sliding off and falling to the floor. The lid popped off and the pearl necklace spilled onto the tile.

Yikes!

Dr. Stapleton reached down and scooped up the necklace with his right hand, letting it dangle from his fingertips. He peered at it, a frown puckering his brow. "These are real."

She swallowed. "I—I know."

"This is for donation?"

"It is. Just clearing out five years of debris." The words tumbled out faster than she meant for them to, and the frown swung her way.

He nodded at the rest of the boxes. "Any other valuable 'debris' in there?"

"No."

"I think I'll put this in my office safe for security's sake." He paused. "And in case you change your mind, you should probably have them appraised, if you haven't already."

"I won't change my mind." She didn't tell him why, but hopefully he could read the conviction in her voice.

He opened the door to the staff lounge and waited while she put the rest of her items onto the table with the others. By now her legs were shaking. She'd hoped to leave everything there without anyone seeing her. But he was right. It was probably better to safeguard the pearls than to leave them lying around, not that she thought anyone on staff would take them. At least the hospital would benefit from her mistake.

Speaking of mistakes, did she really want to sit in his office on a day her eyes had trailed over the muscles in his arms?

Turning to face him, she asked, "What was it you needed to talk to me about?"

"Let's go into my office."

Ugh. There was no getting out of it. And it sounded serious. The last thing she needed right now was "serious."

Garret Stapleton stretched the fingers of his left hand and winced as the act pulled tendons and ligaments that were tight from disuse. He knew better than to try to grip the lock to his safe with the twisted digits. Or a scalpel.

Why were his thoughts heading in that direction today?

He knew. And he'd be damned if he'd sit

back and let someone else make the same mistake he did. He'd heard what had happened with Addy, even though he did his best not to listen to the rumors that floated around. He was sure there were plenty out there about him and his hand.

The "five years of debris" comment made him think that those donations had something to do with her marriage. He shifted the long flat box so that it was under his left forearm as he quickly turned the tumbler right and then left, opening the safe. Then he took the box and slid it on top of a set of files. His files. Files that mapped out what his own errors had cost him.

"Have a seat."

She skirted one of the leather chairs and folded herself into it.

Was she thinner than when he'd first arrived in South Beach three years ago? Or maybe he was imagining things.

"I'm not sure what this is about."

"Aren't you?"

She tipped her head, sending several locks of dark hair cascading over one shoulder.

Maybe calling her into his office to have this conversation wasn't such a good idea after all. But where else could he do it? Certainly not in the staff lounge.

The thumb of his damaged hand scrubbed over his pinkie finger; he wasn't quite sure how to approach this. But if he didn't drop the ax and something happened… "Whenever a doctor's name appears on a chart, it's entered into the system. If the computer finds a disparity between assigned hours and actual hours worked, it sends up a red flag. Do you want to guess how many flags you've generated in the last several weeks?"

"I've had a lot of free time and so I—"

"Try again." He softened the words with a smile. He didn't want to come across as a game warden.

Her chin went up and green eyes flashed. "Why are you asking those questions? If you have a problem with my work, surely that's a matter for Human Resources."

"Normally I'd say you were right and shoot it up to them. But the Emergency Department is the heart of Miami's Grace Hospital. So it's important to me. To the entire hospital."

"My working a few extra hours would help that cause, I would think."

"Yes. One would think. But that's not always the case." He dropped his hand behind the desk, unwilling to use it as an example of what could happen unless he absolutely needed to. "I need you to be at your best."

"I haven't been?"

"You've been a huge asset to this hospital. I'm sure you know that. I don't want one of our best doctors burning out or going elsewhere."

"I have no plans of going anywhere. At the moment, anyway." Her eyes dipped to the edge of his desk before coming back up to meet his.

She *was* thinking about leaving.

"Are you having a problem on the floor? Is someone making life difficult?"

"You mean other than you?" She flashed a grin that traveled all the way to her eyes, crinkling the corners in a way that made his insides clench. But when he didn't smile back, her mouth went back to neutral. "No. Of course not."

"Why the sudden jump in hours, then?" He forced himself to concentrate on the subject at hand. There was no way she could deny that her habits had changed. He might be treading into forbidden territory, but it was his job to make sure this hospital maintained its reputation for providing stellar care.

She hesitated. "I'm going through a personal crisis right now. I just need to work through it, and this is the best way I can think of to do that."

The familiar ring of those words made him tense. He'd gone through a personal crisis of his own a few years back. "Anything you care to share?"

Her head came up, neck turning a dark shade of red. "No. Yes…" There was a long pause, as if she was struggling to figure out a way to tell him something. "I'm divorcing my husband, and things have been difficult."

He sat back in his chair, relief washing through him that her crisis had nothing to do with him. Not that he was happy she was getting a divorce, but the way she'd backed away from him when he'd tried to help her with those boxes had set an alarm off in his head. He'd racked his brain thinking of something he might have done to make her uneasy around him, but had come up empty.

"A divorce."

Okay, so the matter-of-fact way he'd said that had probably sounded crass and unfeeling. He hadn't meant it to. After all, he'd been through a divorce himself and had lived to tell the tale.

"I'm not sure how my hours are a problem as long as I'm not endangering anyone."

He leaned forward. "Sometimes you don't realize you are until it's too late."

"Are we talking about me? Or are we talking about your hand?"

"Excuse me?" Only then did he realize that his injured hand was resting on his desk, the almost useless fingers curled into a ball.

"I'm sorry. I shouldn't have said that."

She was right. She shouldn't have. Except the reason he'd asked her to step into his office had more to do with him than it did with her, and she'd just called him on it. He lifted his hand, turning it over and studying it for a few seconds. "Actually you're right. I did call you in because of this. You've heard about what happened?"

"You know the grapevines. Not much escapes them."

"Ah. I imagine not. And calling you in here isn't personal. It's professional. I don't want to see anyone else ruin their career by working themselves to exhaustion."

"I know my limits."

He smiled to cover the churning in his gut caused by those words. He'd thought he'd known his limits too. How wrong he'd been. "Sometimes we only think we do."

"Believe me, I have no desire to jeopardize something I love more than anything."

He hadn't wanted to either. But once Leticia died…

Swallowing, he stood. "I just wanted to bring it to your attention and ask you to stick to a more sensible schedule."

She laughed and climbed to her feet as well, tossing those wild errant locks back over her shoulder. "I think 'doctor' and 'sensible schedule' are incompatible terms, don't you? Are you going to write me up?"

"Do I need to?"

"I hope not, but that's your prerogative. You can even fire me, if you want. I can always practice somewhere else."

And now he could bring up an earlier thought. "You're already thinking of doing just that, though, aren't you? Leaving?"

There was a long pause. "I hope it won't come to that. My—ex—works for the EMT company that services this area. If he makes things difficult, I might choose to move."

He took a step closer, gratified when she stood her ground this time. "How can I help? The hospital, that is."

"You can't. It's something I have to work through myself. I'll either be able to face him and move on, or I won't. Our parting was not the most amicable in the world."

That made him frown. "Let me know if he causes trouble."

"I think he's caused all the trouble he can. The sooner the divorce goes through, the better." Fingers fiddled with a small gold ball that clung to the delicate lobe of her right ear. Something contracted in his chest.

She allowed her hand to drop back to her side, standing straight and tall. "I'm sure the last thing you want to hear today is someone moaning about their impending divorce."

He glanced back at the safe.

Before he could even give voice to the question, she nodded. "Yes. He gave it to me. And all of those other items as well."

"Ah, understandable. I still think it should be appraised. I can have that done if you'd like."

"It's up to you. I won't want the necklace back no matter what its value."

He glanced at her hand. No rings anymore, but the indentation was still there. "I'm sorry. About your breakup."

"Thank you." She shoved her hands in the pockets of her pants. "Now, if there's nothing else…"

"No. Nothing. Just keep an eye on those hours, okay?"

"I will. Thanks for bringing it to my attention."

Walking over to the door, he held it open and waited as she walked through it. "Oh, and, Dr. Santini."

"Call me Addy."

He nodded. "Addy, then. Thank you for the donations. The hospital appreciates them."

How was that for impersonal? Maybe he'd sounded canned and overly formal, but he didn't like the way he was suddenly noticing little things about her.

"I'm glad someone will be able to use them."

Because she wouldn't. He shut the door and went back around his desk. Giving his damaged hand one last glance, he sat in his chair and tried to lose himself in his work. But Addy's face—and that damned gold earring—kept circling through his thoughts. He hoped she came through her crisis unscathed. And that it wouldn't cost her something a lot more valuable than a set of pearls.

Two days later a piece of mail caught her attention. It was from the hospital. Her breath stalled in her chest. She'd done her best to cut back on her hours, but knew she'd still stayed on the floor longer than she should have.

Sliding her finger under the tab, she was surprised when a single sheet of paper fell out—a handwritten note containing only seven words:

Two thousand dollars appraised—are you sure?

The signature was Garret Stapleton's. A shiver went over her as she sat and stared at his handwriting for a few seconds. Bold strokes crossed those Ts. She touched a finger to one of them, then gritted her teeth.

She knew exactly what he was referring to. The necklace. She wasn't shocked by the price tag. What she was surprised at was that he'd written to her personally. And at the funny twist to her stomach when she'd opened the envelope and realized who it was from.

But at least he hadn't called her back into his office to break the news to her. Their last meeting had made her squirm. Maybe because she'd called attention to his hand, when she hadn't meant to. She'd gone all defensive, trying to deflect his attention to something other than her.

He'd been right to chew her out. But he hadn't needed to. She did know her limits. And she loved her job too much to risk driving while exhausted. Which was why she'd been known to leave her car in the parking lot and take a taxi.

Did he call every single doctor who worked overtime into his office? She didn't think so. Which meant he had seen some kind of warning sign.

She'd heard that the fiery crash that damaged his hand had almost cost his life as well. That thought made her heart ache. He'd been one of the best neurosurgeons in the country. And it had all been snatched away in a split second. He'd then gone from New York City to the shores of South Beach.

Why so far away?

Maybe, like her, he'd felt he needed a change of scenery. A new start. Maybe she needed to do the same—like go from South Beach to New York.

Except she was a Florida girl. Born to a family of Italian immigrants, but a true surfer girl at heart. With her dark hair, she didn't exactly look the part, but she didn't care. Those waves had coaxed her back to the water time and time again.

In fact, she'd met Leo Santini during a surfing contest five years earlier, when she'd been undergoing another crisis—with her mom, this time—and had fallen in love. Looking back, she realized their quick romance had been a desperate attempt on her part to claw her way out of a dark hole, but the effort had backfired. As her mom's condition had continued to deteriorate, their marriage had begun to change gears too. Their surfing trips had dwindled to nothing over the space of a year. She still caught an occasional wave, but Leo had turned in his board for the party scene, something she had no interest in at all. She should have seen the breakup coming. Talk about warning signs. She'd missed them all.

But no more.

Maybe she needed to take her board and head to the beach on Wednesday, her next day off. Then her boss wouldn't be able to say a word about her working too many hours. And maybe it would clear her head and help her find her equilibrium again. Just the thought made her pulse pick up its pace. How long had it been since she'd paddled through the surf, looking for that one great wave?

Too long. That was what she'd do.

Taking a pen, she sat down and crafted her reply to Garret. And she could do it in fewer words than he had: "Very sure." Rather than mail it, she would drop it on his desk. In person. Probably not a good idea, but it was the best way she knew to make the break from Leo definitive, not that it wasn't already.

Shoving the note back into its envelope, she hurried to get ready for the day. Then tonight she would drag her surfboard out of the spare bedroom and check the weather in hopes that conditions—in more ways than one—were perfect.

CHAPTER TWO

THE EMERGENCY ROOM wasn't as busy as it normally was. Sometimes the room was full, medical personnel running back and forth. But it was still early, and the hospital was exceptionally good at triage. His hospital in New York had also had a great quick-response team that could handle multiple trauma cases at the drop of a hat. That attention to skill and speed had probably saved his life after his accident, even though he could only remember bits and pieces of what happened.

Winding his way through the space as he often did on Monday mornings, he mentally kept track of what he saw. He'd made it a habit to visit a different department at the beginning of every workday. Not so much to check up on everyone as to make sure people felt comfortable approaching him. That they felt as if they were being heard.

The last thing he wanted was to be one of those aloof bosses that sat in his office issuing edicts and making sure everyone followed them to the letter. He wanted people to stay at the hospital because they wanted to, because it had an atmosphere that was conducive to sticking around.

Which was why when he'd sensed Addy might want to move on, he'd reacted so strongly. Right?

The emergency-room doctor had caught his attention, and not just because of her hours. Her colleagues talked as if she were some kind of superhero.

Was he sure that wasn't why he was here now? To make sure the hospital's star player wasn't going to burn herself out?

Or was it more personal than that?

Nope. It was Monday. He was simply sticking to routine.

And the envelope he'd found on his desk this morning? She'd arrived even before he had. Had she not heard a single word he'd said?

Nodding to a staff member who made eye

contact, he suddenly wondered if he should have skipped coming down here. He didn't want Addy to think he was seeking her out.

Because he wasn't.

Pivoting on his heel, he almost ran over the very person he was now hoping to avoid.

"Dr. Stapleton." Her wide eyes and breathless tone made him smile. Okay. So maybe it wasn't just him feeling awkward.

"Garret, remember? Everyone else calls me by my given name."

"Oh. Of course." She glanced at the electronic file-storage device still in her hands. "Did you get my note?"

"You mean the one that was lying on my desk when I arrived?"

"I always get here at six." Her quick response was defensive, and her eyes came up to meet his. "I'm off on Wednesday, though. I'm actually planning on surfing."

"Surfing as in the internet?"

Her head cocked sideways. "No. Surfing as in at the beach." Her hand twirled through the air. "In the ocean. Catching waves."

"You—surf?" A quick image of Addy flashed through his skull. A wetsuit? Or, worse, a bikini? He suddenly wished he hadn't asked her to clarify her response.

Up went her brows. "This is South Beach. Doesn't everyone?"

"I haven't taken a survey recently."

She laughed. "Sorry. I just thought that most Floridians… Oh, wait. You're from New York. Sorry. Coming here must have been a big change for you."

His imaginings died a painful death.

"Not as big as other changes." His hand curled next to his side. Why had he just said that? "Both places have a lot of people. And a need for good medical care."

"Of course." She hesitated. "Do you still do consulting at all?"

"Sorry?"

"On cases. I had a head trauma come in the other day and the neurologist on duty was tied up in surgery. It took a little longer to get the patient evaluated than I would have liked."

"Did it change the outcome?"

"The patient didn't make it. But no, the outcome probably would have been the same. But it would be nice to know there's someone else I can call if the need arises."

His jaw tightened. No one at Miami's Grace had asked him that question before. Which was another reason he'd relocated. If people didn't think of him as a neurosurgeon, they wouldn't treat him like one. Did he really want to open that door? Then again, did he want to risk a patient's life by refusing?

"I don't do surgery anymore." Said as if he still could. So why hadn't he said "can't"? Maybe because he hadn't quite faced the fact that he would never again use a scalpel to excise a brain tumor.

Addy frowned. "I realize that. So you're not willing to consult? I just want to be clear so that I don't keep that as an option."

"I'm available if you need me." And just like that, it was out there. Not exactly the way he'd envisioned this conversation going. He'd been all set to chastise her for flouting his request that she moderate her hours, and she'd ended up subtly chastising him for putting himself above their patients.

And she was right. His embarrassment over his hand did drive some of his decisions. Including being the motivating factor behind calling her into his office a few days ago. It had nothing to do with her patients—

or even her well-being—and everything to do with him.

That had to change. Starting now.

"Thank you, Dr.—I mean Garret. You won't regret it."

He already did, but he wasn't going to tell her that. Instead, he nodded at the tablet in her hand. "Nothing neurological this morning?"

"Not so far. Just a gator hunter who shot a hole in his boat. But not before the bullet went through his buddy's foot."

His brows shot up. "Well, I can't remember seeing anything like that at my last hospital."

"You didn't have hunters in New York?"

He thought of the gangland shootings and senseless loss of life. "We did. But they tended to hunt a different kind of prey, and when they shot someone, it wasn't an accident."

"We have that here too." She sighed. "I wish people were different. Kinder."

"There are still some good ones out there." Addy was one of those good ones. He could see it in her work ethic, in the fact that she cared enough about her patients to risk a firm refusal when she'd asked him to consult on cases.

Sometimes, with hospital politics in play, it was easier to just go with the flow and try not to make waves. But that wasn't always what was best for the patient. Here was someone who was not only willing to make waves, but more than willing to swim against the current. Well, surfers had to do that each time they took their boards into the water, didn't they? She was just doing what came naturally.

"Yes, there are. Some of those good ones even come from New York City." She gave a smile that lit up her dark green eyes. Eyes that met and held his for long seconds.

He swallowed. She didn't know him very well. Because if she did, she'd know he wasn't good. Not by a long shot.

But even as he thought it, a warmth seeped into his chest that had nothing to do with a defect in the hospital's climate control system. It had been a while since someone had handed him a compliment that didn't originate with his position at the hospital. He wasn't quite sure what to do with it.

Better just to ignore it. And the way that her smile messed with something inside him.

"So what happened to the man in the boat? The one who was shot?" he asked.

"What didn't happen to him? He fell overboard right after the bullet hit him, dousing his foot with swamp water. Then once back in the boat, he had to bail more water, while his friend drove them back to shore, giving his foot another good dunking." Her smile widened, and it kicked straight to areas best left alone. "So we soaked it with the good stuff, shot him full of antibiotics and updated his tetanus booster."

"Poor guy. And it wasn't even his fault."

"No, it wasn't. I don't think he and his friend are on speaking terms at the moment."

Eyes that had seemed tired and defeated during the meeting in his office now sparkled with life and laughter. He liked the transformation. He tried imagining her with a surfboard under one arm, water streaming down her back, her dark hair wet and tangled from riding in to shore. That was another transformation he'd like to see. And one he wasn't likely to.

"I imagine they're not." He tried to turn

the conversation around before he ended up showing the cards in his hand. Cards he had no business holding at all. "Anyway, about the appraisal. I'll let the person in charge of the auction know about the necklace."

"Good. I was hoping to drop it off without making a big production out of it."

That wouldn't have happened. "We would have put a notice in the staff newsletter asking for information, just in case the donor had no idea as to its value."

Her eyes widened. "I'm glad that's not how things went, then."

"I can understand that. Now. Its presence at the auction isn't going to complicate things for you, is it?"

"I doubt my ex will even attend, so no. It was a wedding gift from him to me, so it's mine to give away. Just like our marriage was his to give away." She wrinkled her nose. "Sorry. I don't know why I said that."

He waited for a nurse to go past, lowering his voice. "He cheated?"

A single nod. "How else do you throw a marriage away?"

He could think of lots of ways. One of which he'd done. Or maybe it had been inevitable, once they'd lost their daughter to a disease that was as relentless as it was deadly.

"Did you try counseling?" He often wondered if he could have saved his marriage if he'd suggested that earlier, before it had been too late. Instead, he'd become unreachable, staying away from home as much as possible.

"Counseling. Right. Would that have been before or after he slept with a mutual friend? Or moved in with her once I discovered what they were doing—had been doing for almost a year."

"Ouch. Sorry." The one thing he'd never done during the whole grieving process was turn to someone else. He'd been so destroyed, so emotionally empty that he'd had nothing to give to anyone else, not even his wife.

None of that had changed with time, and he wasn't sure he wanted it to. The divorce had been his fault—he could acknowledge that now. Some people just didn't deserve second chances.

"It's okay. I knew on some level something was wrong. He was unexpectedly called into work a lot of nights—which now I see probably wasn't the case. Even when he came home, he wasn't really 'there,' if that makes sense. I was dealing with some issues of my own, but if I'd suspected he was that unhappy, I would have done something. Before it got to the point it did."

Garret, on the other hand, had been able to see the slow slide of his marriage and had chosen to do nothing…except put in grueling hours at work. His wife had left him after the accident, while he'd still been in the hospital, saying she wasn't going to watch him throw his life away. She was right. He had been. He'd gotten counseling afterward, had tried to convince her to go with him, but she'd refused. And that had been that. Papers had been waiting for him at the house where they'd raised their daughter. Within weeks he'd sold the place, resigned from his practice, and, after a year of surgery on his hand and physical therapy, the offer from Miami's Grace Hospital had come up and he'd decided to make the move to Florida. But at least his divorce hadn't been as a result of either of them cheating.

"I'm sorry he put you through that."

"It's over. I'm kind of relieved, actually. I'm my own person again."

"A person who surfs in her spare time."

She glanced at him. "You've really never tried it?"

"Nope. Not ever. Is it like snow skiing?"

"Um, no." A quick laugh. Although the falling part might be similar. "Why don't you come with me on Wednesday and see?"

"Excuse me?"

She blinked as if not quite sure what had just happened. "My bad. You're probably not even interested in surfing. Forget I said anything."

Addy was asking him to go to the beach with her? The previous image he'd had began tickling at the edges of his consciousness again. Wetsuit? Or bathing suit? He was a jerk for even letting those kinds of thoughts bounce around his head. "I'm interested in a lot of things."

And that was better?

"So you *want* to go?"

Better that than admit it wasn't surfing that was on his mind.

"Possibly. What time, so I can see if I can juggle my schedule?"

She pursed her lips and studied him, maybe sensing he wasn't being entirely honest with her, then tucked the tablet under her arm and pulled out her phone. She scrolled for a second.

He wasn't sure what she was doing. "Do you want to text me the time?"

"I'm looking right now. Okay, we want low tide, just as it's coming in. Looks like the wind direction will be good as well."

She could have been speaking a different language. "And can you find an actual time somewhere in there?"

"You don't have a board, I take it."

"Not of the surfing variety, no." A flicker of enthusiasm colored her voice and it lit a matching one in him. How long had it been since he'd actually gone anywhere with a woman? It wasn't a date. But it could be fun. He was allowed to have fun, wasn't he?

"It's okay. We can rent a board."

"Whoa." He held up a hand. "I'm not planning on climbing on a surfboard. I was just going to watch."

Like a voyeur.

"You don't even want to paddle out? You don't have to stand up, if you don't want to. You'll be bored if you just sit on the beach."

Doubtful. He turned his scarred hand so

she could see it. "I'm not exactly able to use this the way most people can."

"It'll be fine. Believe me. There are surfers who are missing limbs and still get out there and catch plenty of waves."

He was pretty sure he wasn't going to be one of them, but he didn't feel like arguing the point with hospital staff passing them in the hallway. "So what time would we need to leave?"

"Do you want to meet at the beach or here at the hospital?"

"Beach." The word came out without hesitation. He had no idea if she'd be wearing a bathing suit under her clothes, but he certainly didn't want to meet out front if she was only wearing some kind of cover-up. The gossip chain would have a field day with it. And there was no way he was showing up in board shorts.

"Okay. Well, the tide should be right and the shops open at around ten a.m. Can you swing it if we meet a half hour before that? We'll want to go over some basics. Or you could take a class."

"No. No classes. I don't plan on making

a career out of surfing. But yes, I should be able to make time to come out."

"I think you'll like it." She grinned. "Even if you don't plan on making a career out of it."

She tucked her phone back in her pocket and held up her electronic file. "Well, I'd better get back to something that actually is my career. I'll see you Wednesday at nine thirty?" She suggested the name of a local surf shop as their meeting place.

"I'll be there." He wasn't sure why or how this had happened, but it had. And there was no way he was going to back out and be stuck explaining that his reasons involved a mental tug-of-war over her choice of beach attire. "Anything special I need to bring?"

"Nope. Just yourself and some swim trunks."

Swim trunks. She'd just cemented every reservation he'd ever had about Wednesday's trip.

Instead of swim trunks, maybe he should settle for bringing along what was left of his sanity. Because going to the beach with her was not on his list of smart ideas. In fact, it might just be the dumbest thing he'd ever agreed to. But it was too late to do anything but own his decision…and hope for the best.

Addy pulled her surfboard out of the walk-in closet and ran her hand over the smooth, glossy surface. What had she been thinking asking Garret to go with her? Being with him was hardly going to fill the ticket of taking some time for herself.

She was on edge around him. Had been ever since he'd come to the hospital three years ago. She'd just been careful, because, unlike her husband, her marriage had been important to her.

And look where that had gotten her. Maybe she should have been the first to have an affair.

Her nose crinkled. Not that Garret would have agreed to be her partner in crime. Besides, it wasn't in her to cheat. She was loyal to a fault. It showed in her friendships, and she'd thought in her marriage.

Except that had all been an illusion. Like the perfect wave. It teased and beckoned you to paddle out and see what it was all about. Only it was rarely as glorious as it looked from the shallows. Up close you saw the imperfections and the flaws hidden within the turbulent whitewater.

And a surfboard was incomplete without a wave, just as a marriage was incomplete without trust. That was something she'd never get back again, even if she'd allowed Leo to stay and they'd gone to counseling as Garret had suggested.

And there was the fact that, once discovered, he'd moved right in with his lover.

Oh, well. That part of her life was over. At least it would be once the divorce was final. The sooner the better.

Picking the board up, she set it on the forbidden bed. She gritted her teeth and forced that thought from her mind. Tomorrow if she had time, she'd wax the board up and get it ready for its first outing since her ex had moved out. Garret was right. She had been working too hard. But the alternative was nights like tonight when she had nothing to do but think. And that wasn't good.

All she had to do was get through this evening, and then tomorrow morning she could work her shift, come home again and on Wednesday she'd be out on the water. Not alone, but out there just the same.

She wasn't sure why she'd asked Garret to go with her, but now that she had, she was relieved. Having him there would keep her from backing out and sitting at home brooding the day away. Because she didn't dare show up at work. He would have her head.

It was up to her to show him that she knew how to cut loose and have fun.

Or at least pretend to. Because deep down inside, with everything that was currently going on in her life, she was pretty sure she was going to be anything but a fun date.

No. Not a date. This was an outing. To prove a point.

How did that saying go? Fake it until you make it? Well, she'd better start faking being a fun-time girl, and soon. Or Garret was going to figure out the little secret that she'd been hiding.

What secret was that? That she had eyes for her boss?

She gulped. No, she didn't. And it was up to her to prove that once and for all. If not to him, to herself.

CHAPTER THREE

ADDY SNATCHED THE brochure from the information desk at the front of the hospital in dismay. Oh, Lord, she hoped Leo didn't somehow see this.

And if he did, would it matter?

No, not at all. But she hadn't wanted a lot of attention placed on her. Maybe she'd better make sure she emphasized to Garret that she wanted that donation kept as anonymous as possible. Marching to the elevators, she got in and pressed the button for the fourth floor. She had no idea what she expected him to do about this, but she'd at least like an assurance that her name wouldn't be attached to the pearls.

Going to the door, she knocked and waited for him to respond. When he called for her to come in, she saw that he was with another doctor. Jake Parson, the pediatrician from the first floor.

"Dr. Santini, what can I do for you?"

Oh, so they were back to titles again. She gritted her teeth. Of course they were. It wasn't as if Garret were going to greet her like a long-lost friend. They weren't friends. They were colleagues.

Actually, they weren't. He was her boss, even though it didn't quite work like that in this type of setting.

And she was taking her so-called boss surfing. Another possibly messy situation, if not handled the right way.

Unfortunately, she had no idea what the right way was.

"I didn't know you were with someone. It can wait." Realizing the auction brochure was still in her hand, she tried to shift it so it was hidden behind her leg. She certainly didn't want to talk about this in front of anyone else.

"Jake and I were just finishing up."

Hmmm, okay, so he used Dr. Parson's first name, but not hers?

Maybe realizing he'd been dismissed, the other man stood, throwing her a quick smile as he shook Garret's hand and slid past her with a murmured goodbye.

Once the door closed, Garret came around the side of his desk, nodding in the direction of her hand. "What didn't you want him to see?"

So he *had* noticed.

Now that she was here, she felt kind of idiotic. He more than likely had nothing to do with the marketing division of the hospital's fund-raising events.

"It's the pamphlet for the auction."

"May I see it?"

She gulped. It was obvious he didn't have a stack of them lying around his office. He probably hadn't even seen one yet. Hesitating, she finally pulled the brochure from behind her and held it out for him to take.

A soft whistle sounded as he glanced at the cover. Then he looked up. "I didn't know they were going to put this on the front."

"Neither did I." He'd put the pearls in his safe, so he had to have helped set up the picture, but from his reaction he'd had nothing to do with the photo's placement. "Is there any way you can make sure my name is not attached to them?"

"Is this because of your ex?" He frowned. "I can have the pamphlets recalled, ask them to be redone, if you want. I'm not even sure how they came up with these so quickly."

"No, it has nothing to do with Leo. I'm feeling a little ridiculous even bringing this up here actually. It was just a shock to see the necklace front and center."

"Don't worry. I'll make sure your name isn't listed anywhere. I think the pearls were easier to capture in a simple photo than some of the other donations." He flipped the top page open. "Although they did put some of the cruises on the inside."

He glanced up. "They're not family heirlooms or anything whose ownership can be contested, are they?"

"No. He bought them at a jewelry store." She held up a hand. "And don't ask me if I'm sure again. Once I make up my mind you'll find I don't change it easily."

He made a pained sound in the back of his throat. Before she could ask what it meant, though, he said, "Can I keep this copy?"

"Of course." She gave a wry smile. "There are plenty of them around the hospital, I imagine."

Garret indicated the chair the other doctor had vacated moments earlier. "Have a seat."

"Don't tell me I'm in trouble again. I've tried to keep my hours to pretty much what I've been assigned."

"No, I actually wanted to talk about tomorrow."

Tomorrow?

Oh, the surfing trip. Suddenly she just knew he'd changed his mind about going. A wave of disappointment crashed over her before she could stop it.

You should be glad!

She lowered herself into her chair and braced herself for the news.

"You do realize I'm almost forty, don't you?"

She blinked, not sure where he was going with this. Oh, Lord, he hadn't guessed about that weird little crush she was developing, had he? She was in the middle of a divorce, for heaven's sake. The last thing she should be doing was scoping out his broad shoulders and the way his waist gave way to narrow hips. Except she found herself doing just that. And more.

Even his damaged hand held an odd attractiveness. Maybe because it belonged to him. And this particular "him" had a lot of physical attributes going for him. Attributes she'd noticed against her will.

It was because she was almost single again and Garret was the first hunky man she'd interacted with since her breakup. It had to be that. She *prayed* it was that.

Yes, she'd been looking forward to seeing him on a board and no amount of self-recriminations were going to change that.

Time to ask where he was headed with that particular question before her thoughts went even more haywire. "What does almost being forty have to do with tomorrow?"

If he warned her off him, she was going to slink away, never to be seen again.

"Let's just say I'm a little less sturdy than I used to be."

Sturdy? *Sturdy?*

That was where the crack about his age had come from?

She laughed out loud. Partly in relief. Partly in disbelief.

Up went his brows. "I didn't expect that news to be quite so funny."

"It's not that." She struggled to catch her

breath before it betrayed her in another fit of giggles. "You do realize that I'm only five years away from being forty, don't you? So I could take your words as an insult to all of us who are over thirty."

"You don't look thirty-five."

Oh, God. Did he think she looked older? But how to ask…?

"Do I look *more* sturdy? Or less?"

This time, he was the one to laugh, his chuckle rushing across her like a warm sea current, curling around her toes and almost pulling her feet out from under her. She put her arms on her chair as if the tug might be real.

"Do you really want to know?" he asked.

"I *thought* I did. Surely you have access to the hospital staff members' personnel records."

"I do. And you look much younger, although I realize very few doctors make it out of medical school before their late twenties and then with specializing and residency…"

"Well, I'd like to think I'm pretty sturdy for my age, and I bet you are too. At least if a surfer falls, he lands on a more forgiving surface than, say, a frozen mountain."

"I guess we'll see, won't we?"

The phone in her pocket buzzed. She pulled it out, glanced at the readout and frowned. "It's the nurses' station." She pressed Talk and put it on speaker. "Santini, here."

"Addy, we have a family who's been involved in a house fire. They're en route as we speak. Five people, one adult, four children, one of them an infant."

"How bad?" Addy knew it could be anything from smoke inhalation to third-degree burns.

"Two burn victims, but I don't know the extent of it. ETA ten minutes."

"I'm on my way. Call Dr. Hascup and see if he can come in. And make sure we have some rooms ready." Having a doctor there from the hospital's burn unit was a must.

She ended the call and glanced at Garret, hating to ask since she'd promised she would only request consults on neurological cases.

"I don't know how I can help, but I can at least do triage and direct the nurses."

She sagged with relief. "Thanks. How much use do you have of that hand?" She stood, then realized the question might seem insensitive. But she needed to know before things got hectic.

"I can pick things up with it, but it's more like those claw games that drop, grasp and lift. I can't do anything with it that requires fine motor skills."

Her heart ached at what that admission must have cost him, but there wasn't time to do much more than digest the information. "You can still wield a stethoscope, do visuals and call out treatment orders, so you'll do." It was better not to make a big deal over it.

"I can do that." He stood. "Now, let's go wait for our patients."

He wished he had full use of his hand.

Everyone else was in place outside and knew their jobs. Everyone, except for him.

His screaming nerves almost drowned out the scream of a siren as an ambulance rounded the corner and pulled into the bay of the ER.

He could do this. All he had to do was use his brain. Not his hand.

A blast of hot summer air met him as the sliding doors opened to let him and Addy outside. Despite his feeling like a fish out of water, adrenaline pumped through his system in a steady stream. At least *that* was familiar.

The gurney from the first squad hit the ground with a bump. He went to it as Addy met a second vehicle.

A toddler, who couldn't be more than three years old—and unconscious—came into view, her face streaked with soot. She was clad only in a T-shirt and pull-up diaper, which was understandable since they were at home and the heat index today was closing in on one hundred degrees. The EMT held an oxygen mask over her face. Good. At least she was breathing on her own. "Vitals?"

"BP ninety over sixty, pulse ninety, respiration forty-five. No burns, but she was found in a smoke-filled room."

Right on cue, the girl's diaphragm spasmed in a series of harsh, dry coughs.

Her vitals weren't bad, all things considered.

"Take her inside while I check on everyone else. Anyone critical that you know of?"

The technician nodded. "An infant is pretty bad, and the mom has burns from a pan of grease that caught fire. She tried dousing it with a bucket of water and—"

The flames would have gone everywhere. It played out in his head, and he winced.

The EMT went on, "She has burns mostly on her hands and arms, but luckily the actual fire didn't reach her. A neighbor saw smoke coming out of the window and called 911."

"The other kids?"

"She was holding the baby while cooking. When she threw the water, some of the hot oil hit her, and she must have dropped him. I've heard he's bad, but I had my own patient to take care of, so I'm not sure the extent of it."

The sound of raised voices came from somewhere behind them.

"This is not the time, Leo! Let me treat my patient."

Garret frowned at the EMT, who'd glanced back to where the voices were growing in volume. "Go ahead and take her in. I'll deal with the other patients." Then he headed to where Addy stood, a tech not quite blocking her way, but close enough that it would be awkward for her to try to move around him. Another man who must have been his partner was near the back doors, shifting from foot to foot, obviously not comfortable with the situation. Garret looked the EMT near Addy in the eye, already surmising who he was.

"Is there a problem here?"

The tech—who Garret remembered seeing before—drew himself to full height, but took a step back as if realizing he now had an audience. "No. No problem." He then looked at Addy. "I'll talk to you later."

"I don't think so. And right now I have a job to do. So do you."

Garret's brows lifted. So this was her exhusband. The man was cocky and confident and obviously hadn't expected Addy's negative reaction to whatever he'd said.

The man glanced at him one last time and then moved around to get behind the wheel of the vehicle. The other EMT, who'd been tending to the patient—a boy this time—rattled off the child's vitals. This one was around ten years of age. Once he was done, he murmured, "Sorry about that."

Addy smiled, although it was strained. "Not your fault. Do you mind taking him inside and asking someone to find him an exam room?"

"Not a problem."

She started to walk off as another rescue

squad arrived. Garret's fingers encircled her wrist and gave a reassuring squeeze before releasing his grip. "Hey, you okay?"

"I'm fine. Leo's just a jerk sometimes."

It sounded as if it was more than just sometimes. But there was no way he was going to say that. Plus, Addy was already heading toward the back of the vehicle, stethoscope swinging around her neck, her steps sure and determined.

He caught one more glance at Leo, who threw a scowl his way, but wouldn't hold his gaze.

A fourth ambulance came in, and Garret headed straight for it just as another doctor burst through the emergency-room doors. Lyle Hascup, known for his work in the burn unit, had made it to the hospital more quickly than he expected.

He let Lyle take the lead on what turned out to be an adult female, the one with grease burns to her arms and torso. The woman was in obvious pain, writhing on the gurney, but still asking about her baby in loud tones. Lyle tried to get her to calm down, but she wasn't having it. He glanced at the rescue worker. "Do you know where the baby is?"

"He's following. It took longer to get him stabilized." The man's voice was low. "Head and neck trauma from a fall."

Lyle nodded. "Dr. Stapleton, that is up your alley—do you want to take that one?"

His gut tightened in dread. "Yes. But make sure there's another neurosurgeon in the building, just in case."

"Got it." Then the other doctor was busy with his own patient, barking out orders and running alongside the gurney as they rushed the children's mother inside.

Addy came over. "Have you got the next one? I'm going to go start treatment on the other children. Lyle will do great with the mother."

"I'm good. Go."

The first ambulance pulled out as did the second, which contained Addy's ex. Questions burned in his head, but, as Addy had said, now was not the time. Besides, Addy's relationships were none of his business. Unless it affected her work.

His hand burned with a phantom pain that reminded him that sometimes your private life did bleed into your professional life. He ignored the thought and waited for what seemed like an eternity before finally hearing the telltale wail of the fifth and final siren. The rescue vehicle pulled in and there was a rush of activity in the back as the other squads pulled out to make space for the newcomer.

The back doors swung open and a young EMT jumped down. "We've got a critical patient here. You a doctor?"

Only then did Garret realize he wasn't wearing his lanyard. He'd taken it off in his office so it didn't continually bump the edge of his desk—a constant annoyance.

He also realized the man was staring at his hand, a quizzical look on his face as his eyes swung up again.

"Yes, I'm a neurosurgeon. You can ask anyone inside that building." He didn't go into the fact that he was now basically a desk jockey—a bean counter—who, while retaining his medical license, rarely treated patients nowadays.

"That's good enough for me."

His partner jumped out of the vehicle and came to help lower the gurney as vitals were read. They weren't great. Skull fracture or a brain bleed were at the top of his list. He wouldn't know until he could get a CT scan. He quickly peeled back the baby's eyelids, looking for pupillary reflex.

Neither pupil was blown, which was good, but the right was a little more reactive than the left. He didn't carry a penlight with him anymore as a matter of course. He'd have to borrow one inside, although it would be next to impossible to hold a light while using his good hand to peel apart the baby's eyelids.

He gave a quick listen to his patient's heart, instead, which thankfully sounded strong even if the baby's blood pressure was lower than he'd like it to be. He glanced at the baby's head. No bleeding that he could see in front and the backboard and neck brace prevented him from looking at the back of his skull at the moment.

"Let's get him inside. I want a CT of his head and neck to get a visual on what's going on in there."

They rushed the baby into the emergency room and transferred him from the ambulance gurney to one of the hospital's. He read off orders to the nurse who, in turn, called up to Radiology to let them know they were on their way. "Any idea if there's another parent in the picture besides the mom?"

The EMT shook his head. "I don't know. Another squad was treating her. Maybe check with them."

They were already long gone, but it didn't matter at the moment. He called another nurse over. "Can you see if mom is able to sign a consent form? I'm taking him upstairs."

"I'll get on it and call you when it's done." It was gratifying not to have anyone question his requests, not that he'd thought they would. But he had expected more sideways looks or raised brows. He'd gotten none.

By the time they arrived in the imaging department, the consent form had been signed and scanned into the system. "The mother's pretty upset," the nurse said.

"Understandable. I'll let you know as soon as we have an idea on…" he glanced at the form on the electronic pad "…Matthew's condition. How are the other kids?"

"Mostly smoke inhalation. One broken finger from the melee right after the fire broke out. It's already been splinted. They'll be admitted overnight to watch for anything else."

Another nurse came over. "ER just called up. The mother is single and says the dad is out of the picture. She's having someone call her mom, who's in Michigan."

Michigan. Hell, that might as well be the other side of the world. If they couldn't find a relative or friend who could watch the kids as they were discharged, what would happen to them while their mother was in the hospital recovering?

That really wasn't his call. And right now, he had a little boy to worry about.

The imaging technician made quick work of getting the baby into the machine. Since he was still unconscious there were no issues with keeping him still, a very small blessing. All in all, the procedure took less than five minutes.

While a nurse waited with the baby, Garret looked at the scans, noting immediately there was indeed a basilar fracture, which would make sense since the mother had reportedly dropped the baby when the grease had flared toward her. The force of his head striking the hard tile floor could have caused a linear fracture like the one he saw on the film. He didn't see any areas of brain compression that might indicate an active bleed. Another good sign.

The fact that he hadn't gotten burned as well was a testament to the way his mother had reacted to the fire by turning away. It could have been worse. Much worse. It didn't look as if he'd need to call in an actual surgeon. They could treat conservatively and get a good result, hopefully. The baby's eyes were darkening underneath, meaning he would have two good-sized shiners by morning, but that was also normal with this particular type of fracture.

No neck injuries that he could see on the scans, so they could take the collar off and find a bed in the pediatric ICU area so he could be watched.

He quickly wrote up orders for Matthew's care and made sure there was a room available. The baby's vitals were stabilizing, and he was starting to stir. And fuss. No wonder. He had to have a massive headache. Garret touched a finger to the back of the baby's hand. "Don't worry, little guy. We're going to take good care of you and hopefully get you reunited with your mom very soon." He made a note to hand off the case to another of the hospital's neurologists. He would see who was due to come through to do rounds in the morning, since it was already getting late, judging from the sky. But for tonight, he would check on the baby before he left the hospital.

Speaking of which, he wanted to peek in on the mom as well. Glancing down at his curled fingers, he hoped her hands would fare better than his had.

By the time he made it back to the emergency room, the rooms had been cleared out and there was no sign of Addy. Maybe she'd left for the day. He glanced at his watch, surprised to find it was almost nine in the evening. He was supposed to meet her in the morning for the whole surfing thing. He'd done his best to think of a way to weasel out of it, but had come up with nothing.

Just as that thought hit, she rounded a corner and stopped dead as if shocked to see him. Had she thought of turning in the other direction only to realize it was too late? It was what he might have done, given the opportunity.

He decided to speak up first. "How are they?"

"I was just about to ask you the same question. I was on my way to the elevator to check on the baby."

"Matthew."

"Sorry?"

Why had he said that? "The baby's name. I saw it on the consent form."

"Ah. How is he?"

He nodded toward the chairs at a nearby waiting area, noting the way her eyes widened.

"He made it, didn't he? Grace will be devastated, if something happened."

"He has a skull fracture, but nothing that time can't heal."

Addy sagged into one of the chairs. "Thank God. Grace kept saying she would never forgive herself for letting go of him."

"If she'd held on, he might have shielded her from the flames, but would have gotten the worst of it himself." Garret sat beside her. "I take it you've heard about how the others are?"

"They're all in rooms for the night. We juggled some patients so we could keep the family as close together as we could. Two of them will be on oxygen for the duration of the night. One of them could probably be discharged, but—"

"There's nowhere for them to go. Yeah, I heard that from one of the EMTs. I take it the grandmother is making arrangements to come down?"

"Yes. Grace said she found a flight. She should be here later this evening."

"How is she, by the way? The burns?"

"Believe it or not, she's fairly lucky. She has several partial thickness burns. Most of the ones on her arm and neck, though, are superficial. But there are two areas on her hands that are deep."

Also known as second-degree burns, partial thickness burns affected the first two layers of the dermis.

He swallowed. "Her hands. Nerve damage?"

"Possibly, but they'll keep an eye on them and watch for infection. It could have been a whole lot worse."

He leaned back, expelling the air in his lungs. "I just got done saying that after looking at Matthew's CT scans. Did they lose their house?"

"No. One of the EMTs told me the fire was

contained quickly. One wall in the kitchen has some fire and water damage, and smoke, obviously, but it could have been—"

"Much worse." He laughed.

She smiled and twisted in the seat to look at him. "So how does it feel to play doctor again?"

Play doctor? He glanced sharply at her.

"It feels strange. And kind of nice." He was going to avoid thinking about any other connotation behind her words. "I've missed it."

"You're still a doctor, Garret. You realize that, don't you?" She touched his injured hand, sending a burst of heat through it. The friction from her fingers was almost unbearably intimate. "This..." she brushed her skin against his once again "...doesn't affect who you are or what's in your head. In your heart."

He gritted his teeth, fighting the tension growing inside his belly and sweeping to other areas.

"It affects what I can hold in my hand, though, doesn't it?" Even he could hear the bitterness in his words. "My whole life changed in the space of a few seconds."

When he looked in her face he saw a wide

range of emotions: concern, dismay and, finally, compassion. What he didn't see was what he dreaded the most: pity. But even without that, he could guess what the next words out of her mouth would be before she'd even given voice to them.

"What happened, Garret? To your hand?"

CHAPTER FOUR

THE WAITING ROOM was still empty; the day-to-day visitors in this area had gone home for the most part. Addy loved it when the hospital was like this. Quiet and almost peaceful. You could almost forget there were life-and-death battles raging inside these halls.

The battle going on in Garret's head right now might not be life or death, but she could tell he was trying to decide how much to tell her. She knew he'd been in an accident that had damaged his hand, but she didn't know how it had happened, although she'd heard some vague rumors about his daughter dying and him going off the deep end.

"I was in a car accident four years ago. I was coming off a fourteen-hour shift, and I was tired." He rubbed a hand across his brows, his mouth twisting. "I fell asleep behind the wheel."

Something in her heart twisted, that meeting in his office taking on a whole new meaning that was impossible to ignore. Hadn't she driven home desperately tired before—found her eyelids sinking and had to jerk herself back to wakefulness?

"I didn't know."

"I'm surprised, actually. I thought hospital grapevines were notorious about digging up the dirt on everyone."

"Hard to do that on someone who's just as notorious about his privacy. I heard you had a daughter who died. I'm sorry."

"We lost Leticia to leukemia at age ten."

His daughter had been ten? He must have married young. But it would be just as devastating to lose a child no matter what the age. "I'm sorry."

She had to ask. "Is this why you wanted me to cut back on my hours?"

"Yes. I wouldn't wish this—" he lifted his hand "—on my worst enemy."

"I can understand that. But there's still so much you can do, Garret. You showed that today as you were treating that baby. You could teach. I've heard stories about how talented a surgeon you were—still are."

"I can't do surgery at all."

Her head tilted. "Yes, you can."

Reaching over, he used his damaged hand to grasp hers, tried to raise it off the arm of the chair. He made it up a few inches before losing his grip. The laugh he gave was humorless. "See? Nothing more than a claw game. So do you want to rethink that?"

She leaned forward, forcing him to meet her eyes. "You can still do surgery. In here, Garret." Her fingers lifted to touch his temple. His skin was warm, his dark hair tickling the back of her hand. She swallowed back a rush of emotion. "And then you can share that knowledge with medical students. You have so much to offer them."

"No. Absolutely not." His eyes darkened, pupils swallowing his brown irises.

"But why?"

He got to his feet as if he couldn't stand her touching him. Why had she even done that? And how stupid was she for discussing this with him? She barely knew the man. He worked in the same hospital, but that didn't

mean they were automatically friends or con-
fidants.

In fact, it appeared he resented her personal questions, as well he should. She owed
him an apology.

"I'm sorry. I had no business asking you
about your private life."

He didn't answer for a minute, a muscle in
his cheek pulsing in the sudden silence. He
finally blew out a breath. "I'm the one who
should apologize. I overreacted. It tends to
be a touchy subject."

And yet he said he missed practicing medicine. Why wouldn't he want to share his love
of it with others? She would probably never
know.

"I pried where I shouldn't have. It won't
happen again."

He brushed off her words with a wave of
his hand. "No harm done. I think I'll go up
and check on my young patient and make
sure he's okay before I head out for the night."

"Okay. Good night."

She wasn't sure how to ask if they were
still on for tomorrow. They probably weren't.
She wouldn't blame him if he'd changed his
mind about going after that tense exchange.

Well, she'd simply show up at the beach at the specified time and place. If he came, great. If he didn't, she would still catch some waves on her own. In fact, it might even be better that way. No distractions. And no opportunities to put her foot back in her mouth.

Heaving a sigh that felt heavier than an elephant, she waited until he was out of sight and then got out of her chair and made her way through the exit doors. The image of Garret driving home late one evening and waking up in the hospital was not going to be easy to erase. But she'd better at least try. Because he'd made it very clear that he did not want to talk about his personal life with anyone.

And most definitely not with her.

It was a typical balmy South Beach morning. Addy propped her board against the rail of the surf shop and glanced at her waterproof watch—one of the few times she actually wore one nowadays, since she couldn't carry her phone into the surf. Nine twenty-nine. He wasn't coming. Why that sent a wave of disappointment sloshing over her, she had no idea. But it did. She'd told herself she didn't want him to come and watch her surf, but it was a lie. Because unlike him, she did like to help people explore new things.

She'd never officially taught anyone to surf, and she had no idea if Garret would even want to try, but she had helped colleagues who'd had an interest in learning get the basics.

Oh, well. It didn't look as if that—or anything else—was going to happen. He was a no-show.

Picking up her board, she started to move toward the sand of the nearby beach when she heard her name. Her feet quit moving.

Garret!

She shut her eyes and tried to stop the sudden gallop of her heart. This was ridiculous. She was not going to go all starry-eyed.

Ha! Too late.

Well, then, she wasn't going to let him know how glad she was that he'd decided to come.

She turned and there he was, tanned legs emerging from solid black board shorts. The white drawstrings at the top of his waistband teased her eyes for a split second before she jerked her gaze upward. She decided then and there she wasn't going to try squirming into the light wetsuit she'd stuffed in her beach bag. That would be a fiasco. She'd just wear her bikini, as plenty of other surfers in Florida did.

The racerback top was snug enough to stay in place no matter how big the wave. Besides, it was pretty obvious that Garret hadn't brought much with him, other than himself.

And that was plenty.

Her mouth gave a slight twist of exasperation. She needed to get her thoughts under control.

Sporting a black nylon exercise shirt, he had a gray beach towel draped over his left arm. His injured hand was hidden in the folds. On purpose? And there was not a surfboard in sight.

Then again, she hadn't expected him to buy a board just for this excursion, but the idea of him sitting on the beach watching her ride the waves made her swallow.

Oh, no. If she was surfing, he was surfing. Or at least he was going to paddle out there with her.

"They have board rentals at the kiosk."

"I'm not sure—"

"I am. Sure, that is. You need to try."

"Has anyone ever told you that you have a one-track mind?" He smiled, and the transformation from the grim reaper figure of last night snatched the breath from her lungs.

Ugh! She needed to be careful. It would be a long time before she let another pretty face charm her into giving a piece of her heart away. Leo might be over and done with, but the repercussions of their relationship were not.

Only Garret's face wasn't pretty. It was rugged. With touches of danger around the edges. She'd seen a little bit of that last night when she'd probed too close to a painful area.

"Maybe a time or two." She smiled back.

Keep it light and friendly, Addy. Steer clear of any flashing caution lights.

Like that drawstring? Oh, yes, exactly like that. She didn't let herself blink for a few seconds, afraid if she did, her pupils would head straight for—

"I have no idea what size," he said.

Addy froze.

Size? Don't even think it!

She took a deep breath. "It's fine. I'll help you choose."

Telling the man at the desk what they were looking for in a voice that wasn't quite steady, she waited while he pulled a teal board from a walled-off storage area.

"Are you sure this is a good idea?"

She wasn't sure at all anymore, but hadn't she said she was going to fake it until she could make it? That flip advice suddenly didn't sound so smart after all. "Don't worry. It'll be fun. You'll see."

Fun. She had no idea how she had ever thought coming here with him would be anything short of a disaster.

"The last time I heard that, my dau—" Any hint of a smile disappeared. His throat moved a time or two, then went still. "It was a teacup ride. And it was not a good idea."

It would have been funny, except for the obvious pain on Garret's face.

All the sexy thoughts she'd had moments ago vanished, replaced by a terrible ache in her chest. She couldn't imagine what he'd gone through losing his daughter, even though she'd experienced her share of loss in the emergency room. Every single child she was unable to save was imprinted on her brain. The names were long forgotten, but the faces weren't. Nor were the tears shed by those who'd loved them.

And then there was her mom.

And this was not what she wanted to think about right now. "Well, this is nothing like a teacup ride. It's more like Mr. Toad's Wild Ride."

"Mr. Toad's what?"

"It's a ride the theme park in Florida is famous for." She glanced at him for a second. "It doesn't go in circles, but it does go up and then plummets, and has plenty of stops and starts to keep you busy. That's what I'd compare surfing to."

"That's what I was afraid of."

She laughed, and the atmosphere changed in an instant. Once he'd paid his rental fee, he hefted his board onto his shoulder, his bicep flexing in a way that made her tummy tighten. Just like that day at the hospital.

It wasn't the way people normally carried their boards, and it broke the unwritten etiquette about how to transport them, but it worked. And it looked good. Very good.

Or maybe it was just him. Several women's heads had already swiveled in their direction. Only then did she realize that he was using his bad hand to hold the board in place. So he could use it, when he had to. He tended to try to keep that hand out of sight. At least she'd noticed him doing that in his office and when they were caring for the house-fire victims.

She wondered if he was even aware of it. But the hand, riddled with red and white scars from his burns, was able to curl perfectly around the rim of the board.

A claw game.

If he didn't have to flex and extend his fingers, then they were useful.

To avoid staring more than she already had, she hiked her beach bag onto her shoulder and tucked her own board under her arm. She then led the way to the beach where some other surfers were already riding the waves. It looked like the perfect day to learn. The waves weren't all that high. Normally that would be a disappointment, but in this case she was glad of that fact. He'd talked about his hand being a detriment, but she didn't know how true that would be when it came to surfing. If he was self-conscious and worried about how it might appear to others, then it might make him clumsy about manipulating his board in the water. She stopped halfway to the ocean, set her board and beach bag down and spread her towel on the sand.

"We're a long way out, aren't we?"

"It's low tide. We don't want to come back and find out the water stole our clothes, do we?"

A muscle twitched in Garret's cheek as he set his own things down next to hers. "No. We wouldn't want to find our clothes gone."

Oh, Lord. She hadn't exactly worded that very well, had she?

Too late. She was picturing them—a very naked them—standing on the shore, muttering about their missing garments. Garret's shorts were floating, those pesky drawstrings waving goodbye as they traveled away on ocean currents.

Trying to quickly change the subject, she sat on the towel and kicked off her sandals. "Are you ready for a crash course on riding the waves?"

"I didn't think I had a choice back at the kiosk."

"You don't. I'm only here because you wouldn't let me stay at work." She shook her head to keep him from making a comment.

"And you were right. I have been working too many hours. I'll try to do better."

"Your ex. Is he causing trouble?"

She rolled her eyes. She'd been hoping he wouldn't bring up the scene outside the ER. "He is, but I can handle him."

"Are you sure? I can intervene, if you want."

"Not necessary, but thank you. He decided he wants to do counseling."

Garret shot her a quick look. "And will you?"

"It's not the kind of counseling you're thinking of. It's divorce counseling called *The Amicable Parting of Ways*. It's his new girlfriend's idea. She and I were once friends, and she's decided she wants to kiss and make up."

"What did you tell him?"

"I told him no. I have no interest in trying to stay friends with either of them. I'm sorry our messy split was put on public display in the hospital loading zone, though."

"Not your fault at all." He dropped his own board onto the sand and put his towel next to hers. Staring out over the ocean, he grimaced. "I'm pretty sure I'm not going to make a good surfing student."

"I bet you'll surprise yourself. Let's go ahead and get started."

Since she'd already slathered herself in sunscreen just so she wouldn't have to do it in front of him, she stood and hesitated for a second. But there was no way she was going into the water with her shorts and T-shirt on. And she wasn't going to turn her back on him like a shy schoolgirl either. This was Florida, and they were both adults. They'd both been married—were both doctors—so they'd seen the human body thousands of times. It was no big deal.

Taking a deep breath, she stripped her shirt off and then shimmied out of her shorts, standing in front of him in just her red bikini.

She thought the color drained out of Garret's face, but he quickly got up as well and yanked his shirt over his head in one quick motion, using his good hand.

Her lungs seized, and her heart tripped over itself several times before tumbling into a chaotic rhythm she was powerless to control.

And that was when Addy knew she was in trouble. Big, big trouble.

* * *

Garret tried to replicate the fancy move Addy had shown him on the beach. But while she was able to scramble to her feet with easy grace and ride the wave in, he'd swallowed so much salt water that he was pretty sure the ocean levels had dropped an inch or two.

Dragging himself in to shore, he carried his board the way he'd seen Addy and others do it—under his arm. It was kind of a necessity, since the tether attached to his ankle didn't stretch far enough to put the board back on his shoulder. When he reached where she stood he groaned. "I am never going to be a surfer. I still can't get it."

"The pop up isn't easy." She dropped her board onto the beach, then pushed aside some sand so her fins were buried. "Let's practice it again."

Practice? He'd watched her, but there was no way he'd been willing to copy her. He'd barely been able to keep his knuckles from dragging on the ground as he'd tried to pay attention. The way her back arched on the board put his senses on alert. Not that they weren't already.

He glanced around the beach, which

seemed even more crowded than it had a half hour earlier. "I don't think so."

"Come on, people do it all the time. It's how they teach surfing. Afraid someone will look at you?"

He was sure people were already looking. But not at him. At her. That fire-engine-red bikini she had on had set a few embers burning, and the longer they were out of the water, the harder that was to conceal. The top was some kind of weird halter-top-looking thing with straps that gathered together in the back. But it fit like a glove and was somehow sexy as hell.

It was absurd and maddening but there was absolutely nothing he could do about his reaction to it. He'd tried.

Hell, he'd done everything he could think of. His libido was going all caveman on him and it was driving him crazy, which was where his knuckle-dragging thoughts from a few minutes earlier came from. All he wanted to do was to stay in the water until it was time for them to get dressed and go home.

And then he was never going surfing with her again.

"Not exactly."

"Okay, I'll show you again. Watch the way my legs move."

Not a problem. He was watching her legs and everything above them. And if she kept phrasing things that way, he was going to have to go stand waist deep in the ocean for his own sanity.

And she never gave him a chance to refuse, lying down on her board in one smooth move. "Okay, so you've already paddled out and have now turned to face the shore. You're in the center of the board and your feet are on the tail." She arched her back, and there it went again. The swallowing of saliva. The inner panic that he was going to lose it.

"There'll be a moment where you feel yourself picking up momentum as the wave catches you. Put your hands under your chest and push hard, and kind of jump onto your feet."

She demonstrated in one fluid move, her hips moving in time to an imaginary wave. "Now you're riding it, all the way in to shore."

This was bad. Very, very bad.

Before he'd totally recovered, she went back into a prone position on the board and showed him all over again. "And that's the pop up. If that doesn't work for you, you can push off, get your back knee under you, plant your front foot and stand. Whichever method, it's got to be fast. Explosive, even. If you take too long getting to your feet, you'll fall off. Basically, your front foot should end up where your chest was on the board."

The last way looked a little more doable on a moving board. "I can try that kneeling method."

Anything to stop those long limbs from demonstrating again. And keep her from talking about riding anything.

"Great. Let's try it again, then."

Once in the water, he shook his head. Hell, whether he got upright on the board or not, her moves were going to haunt him long into the night.

He paddled beside her, and tried to concentrate on what she'd told him. There! A wave was forming in the distance. Following her lead, he turned around and started paddling, keeping his chin up.

Damn. There it was. That push she'd talked about. In one quick move he shoved himself onto a knee and suddenly found himself standing sideways on his board. For all of a second, before he dived headfirst into the water. Again.

But he'd stood!

"Plant your feet further apart," she yelled when he came up. "You almost had it."

Three tries later, he was on his feet, shaky as hell, but he stayed up, trying to follow the quick movements of his board. This time when he jumped off it was on his terms.

"Great job, Garret! You did it!" Her smile was wide and excited, and she held up her right hand for a high five. He smacked her palm with his, their fingers twining together for a second or two as a feeling of victory stole over him. He'd actually done it. He'd surfed. Something he'd never done in his life—never had a desire to do. But it was exhilarating and his hand hadn't given him much of a problem at all. Flattening it on his board to push himself up was painful, so he'd allowed it to curl in on itself instead, as he did when he did push-ups. It had worked like a charm.

Well, not exactly, but at least it hadn't kept him from doing what he wanted to do. As it had with surgery.

He'd had an ortho guy tell him he could probably help stretch his tendons so he was better able to open his hand, but it would never be the way it once was. He'd opted not to have additional surgery. As long as he could zip his pants and button his shirt, it would have to do. And there was always the possibility that surgery would make things worse, if there were complications.

They released their hold on each other and carried their boards onto shore. Addy released the clip holding her hair back and shook it out as they sat down, finger-combing out the tangles and adjusting the bottom edge of her bikini top. "Do you like it?"

His mind blanked out for a second before he realized she wasn't talking about the curls she'd set free or her swimwear. Lord, he could see the hard press of her nipples.

He shut his eyes for a second.

"Garret?"

Oh. The surfing. Had he liked it?

He actually had. He couldn't remember the last time he'd high-fived someone. And the way she'd gripped his hand afterward…

Yes. He'd liked it.

"I did. Thank you for asking me to come."

He undid the Velcro tether around his ankle and leaned back on his elbows, the heat from the sun jump-starting the drying process. "I may have to look into buying a board."

"Seriously?" Her brows went up and a smile hovered around the corners of her mouth.

"Seriously." He liked making her smile. Liked her jubilation over his successful ride on that last wave.

And that should worry him. Everything about today should worry him. He'd screwed up one woman's life, making her walk a lonely path before she finally threw in the towel. He didn't need to repeat that with anyone else.

But it was one day. One great day, where he could leave his dark past and his mistakes behind. It wasn't likely to last, so why not enjoy it to its fullest?

She turned toward him, face tilted upward to catch the sun. Her hair pooled on the ground behind her. His hand ached to touch it to see what the salt did to those shiny locks.

"How is Grace and her family?" she asked. "Have you heard?"

It took a minute to drag his thoughts from

touching things to where they needed to be. "The house-fire victims?"

"Yes."

"I actually went in to the hospital to check on Matthew and his mom before coming to the beach. It's why I was a few minutes late. They're doing really well. The grandmother arrived just as I was leaving, so Grace will have some help with the kids when they go home."

"That's great." She paused. "I actually thought you were standing me up."

"If Matthew hadn't been doing well, I might have. But I would have called to let you know." He frowned. "You really thought I wouldn't come?"

"I wondered. After last night—"

His head tilted sideways. "The argument with your ex?"

"No, your reaction to my suggestion about teaching."

He'd had a pretty strong reaction to that. He'd realized almost as soon as he'd left that he'd been abrupt to the point of rudeness. He'd already apologized, but felt the need to do it again. "Sorry. I've just had several people ask me the same thing. You know the old saying, don't you? 'Those who can, do—those who can't, teach.'"

Her frown was as big as her earlier smile had been. "You can't seriously believe that. How do you think people get through medical school? If there were no teachers, no one would ever become a doctor."

"No, I don't believe that philosophically. But in practice? In my case, it's true. And I just haven't been willing to face that—to accept it as my new reality."

"Is it such an awful reality?"

"No. I guess not." Being the administrator of a teaching hospital had seemed like a good thing when it had been offered to him, but was he really happy doing what he did? He wasn't sure. Three years wasn't really long enough to make a determination on that. "Maybe at some point I'll think about it."

"If you'd had a resident working with you on Matthew's case, he could have learned some valuable tips about skull fractures and how to assess and treat them. Instead, you handed him off to a veteran neurosurgeon and no one learned anything."

"Point taken." She was as blunt as she was beautiful.

She put a hand on his wrist, the clinging grains of sand pale against her tanned skin. "I didn't mean that to come out as harsh as it did. You just have so much talent."

"I could have been a complete hack, for all you know."

"I heard the hospital in New York didn't want to let you go. They don't fight a resignation unless they consider you valuable."

Yes, they had fought it. They'd offered him a huge incentive to stay, even though they knew he would probably never operate again.

"If I hadn't left, I never would have learned how to surf, though."

In her case, those who could also taught. And being at the beach with her had been fun.

"Well, there is that. Are you glad you came?"

He couldn't remember the last time he'd actually enjoyed an outing with a woman. Certainly those last months with his ex-wife had been pretty excruciating. She'd been right to leave him. He knew there was no going back and fixing things. Nor did he want to. He'd been an ass. And now that he knew he had it in him, he didn't trust himself not to repeat some of those mistakes.

So he needed to tread carefully with Addy, because something was brewing that he didn't quite understand. That he didn't quite want to stop.

"I am. I had a good time."

"I'm really glad. I think we both needed to get away for a while."

Her words were low, fingers still on his wrist. He let them stay there, unwilling to pull away as more and more of that uncertainty began swirling inside him.

"I know I did."

Her eyes centered on his. There was a dot of sand on her chin, and he couldn't stop himself from reaching over to brush it away with his thumb. Her skin was soft and warm, the ocean water having dried to a fine film.

If he kissed her, would she taste of salt?

Was it "if" he kissed? Or was it—when?

"Garret?"

"Sand."

"I'm sure it's on more than just my chin."

Was that an invitation?

His gaze skated down the line of her throat, the indent of her waist, the curve of her hip.

And yes, she had sand clinging to her arms. Her legs. Her feet.

And suddenly he knew. He was *going* to taste her skin.

He leaned forward and stopped within an inch of his goal. He waited for her to pull away or make a move that said she didn't want this. She studied him for a few seconds and they hovered. Person to person. Mouth close to mouth.

Before he could finish assessing her reactions, or decide if he would actually go through with it, she did the last thing he expected. Addy closed the gap and kissed him first.

CHAPTER FIVE

Garret's mouth was warm. No, it wasn't. "Warm" was too ambivalent a word. It was hot, burning hers. He'd stayed still for a split second when her lips touched his, but surely he'd been headed in this direction when he'd moved so close. She'd just jumped in quicker than he had. Mainly because she'd been afraid he was going to back out. She'd been wanting to kiss him ever since she watched him strip off his shirt before they hit the water. Each moment of their lesson had inflamed that need, as had the brief moments she'd caught him looking at her.

God, she really did have a crush on him.

Did it matter, if he felt the same way?

When she'd demonstrated the pop up on her board, she'd watched color creep up his neck and into his face and wondered if it was pooling in any other areas of his body.

It had been driving her crazy.

It was still driving her crazy.

His hand came up and slid beneath her hair, curving around her nape, his thumb stroking the side of her neck in a way that made her shudder. Heat rushed through her, winding around and around until she was encased, held prisoner by her own need.

Her tongue slid along the seam of his lips, and his thumb ceased its movements. She settled closer, desperate for him to touch her.

They were on a public beach, for God's sake. He couldn't just lay her back and yank off her bikini bottoms. Even if she ached for him to do just that.

Without warning, Garret jerked back, the movement so sudden that she almost fell on top of him.

He shut his eyes, his chest rising and falling with a ragged sound that was nothing like the muted sounds of the ocean around them.

She had no idea what made him pull away, but, God, she was glad he had. She'd been on the verge of making a fool out of herself. A very, very big fool.

What had gotten into her? Hadn't she let herself get involved with Leo after barely knowing him? Had she learned nothing from that experience?

Garret probably thought she was overeager—maybe even desperate. A hot wash of embarrassment poured over her.

She didn't want his eyes to open, because when they did—

"Ah, hell, Addy. I have no idea where that came from."

An apology, right? Dear Lord, she hated that he was sorry. Hated that she was shaking like a leaf, unable to capture any of the words rattling around in her head.

Finally, she sat up, dragging her fingers through her tangled mass of hair. She counted to three in an effort to compose her thoughts then sucked down a deep breath, reaching for the first excuse she could find. "It's the ocean. It gets to you."

"Is that what it was?"

Was she that desperate to explain her behavior? Evidently, because the look he gave her was a mixture of doubt and relief. She was the one who'd planted her lips on his.

She could only hope what she'd said was true, that the ocean was actually to blame.

"It was on my part." Said as if she truly believed what she was saying.

He planted his elbows on his knees, sending her a frown. "I didn't come out here hoping something like this would happen. I hope you know that."

Was he worried she'd file a sexual harassment report with the hospital? That made her cringe, more heat piling on top of the previous batch in her face.

"I'm the one who asked you to come, remember."

"I do, but—"

She gulped. This was ridiculous. "Listen, I know you didn't come here with anything in mind. I didn't either. It just—happened. People kiss all the time. It's not a big deal." It was to her, since she didn't actually "kiss all the time." But he didn't need to know that. "There's no reason we can't just put this behind us, is there?"

She wasn't exactly sure she could do that, but she was desperate to get back to the place they'd been before any of this had happened. To kill the growing awkwardness between them.

This was nothing more than a day on the beach where there were skimpy suits, tanned skin and impulses that drove men and women to have sex.

Sex.

That was not going to happen.

As impulsive as kissing him had been, spending the night with him would be a hundred times worse.

She was not going to jump into a relationship again. Especially not in response to a crisis the way she'd done the last time. Her mom's condition had driven her into Leo's arms. She wasn't going to let her marital breakup drive her into someone else's arms. Especially not her boss's.

Not that there was any chance of that happening.

"No, there's not."

At first she thought he'd read her mind and was responding to her thoughts. Then she realized he was simply answering her earlier question.

"Good." She wrapped her arms around her knees and looked out at the ocean. "It was simply the euphoria of perfecting the timing on your pop up."

"Why the hell do they have to call it a pop up, of all things? Couldn't they have come up with a better term?" His voice sounded strained.

She smiled, having a pretty good idea why the description was bothering him. And she could have done a better job with her phrasing.

Perfecting the timing on your pop up?

That could definitely be taken to mean something entirely different.

Right now, she was very glad she was a woman. Her insides might be tied up in knots, but at least there wasn't any outward physical evidence of her thoughts.

Making a conscious effort to edge the conversation back onto neutral territory, she said, "You've never heard of popping up on your board?"

"I barely knew what a surfboard was before, much less tried to use one."

Smiling, despite herself, she said, "Well, now you can put a new skill on your résumé."

"Popping up. New skill. Right."

Maybe she could put that on her résumé

as well. Having urges pop up where they weren't welcome. Maybe that was her cue to get out of there before she did anything else stupid. "You never know. And as fun as this has been, it looks like most of the surfers are giving up. The tide has come in too far for the waves to be any good."

Glancing at how the water was lapping several yards further inshore than it had been, she knew it was the truth. But it was more than that. She needed to escape, to have time to process what she hoped was a simple case of the atmosphere getting the best of her. "I guess it's time to turn in my rental board."

"You can stay if you want." A quick glance at her watch showed it was almost twelve fifteen. They'd been out here for almost three hours. And in spite of her doubts about what had happened, she'd had a good time. "I need to go home and catch up on some fun things, like laundry and cleaning."

"You won't go into the hospital today."

"Not unless I'm called in."

He nodded. "Good."

"What about you? Are you taking the rest of the day off?"

"Yes. I do learn from my mistakes."

He could have been referring to his accident. Why, then, did she feel as if that had been directed at what had happened between them a few minutes ago? Well, that was fine. She would learn from her mistakes as well. Like never watching him undress ever again.

That meant no more beach outings. And she was going to have to be okay with that.

Because to do anything else was inviting disaster on a whole new level. And with Leo standing as a bright reminder of what could happen when she let herself off her leash, she needed to watch her step.

So what did she do now?

First thing was there would be no more outings with Garret. She was making a promise to herself. Unless it was related to work, it was off-limits. Everything was to be business as usual. No more kissing. No more surfing. No more anything.

No matter how hard that promise might be to keep.

A week after the kiss, Garret stood with Grace and the rest of her children at the front entrance of the hospital. They were being discharged. Actually three of the kids had gone home with Grace's mom a day after the fire.

Repairs to the house were well under way, so life would soon get back to normal for them. Well, maybe not completely normal. It would take a while for Grace to come to terms with dropping Matthew. Right now, her mom held the baby, even though the burns on Grace's hands and arms were healing. But it was something she would work through, hopefully.

Kind of like he was working through what had happened between him and Addy on the beach.

Addy had asked him to call when the family was released so she could come see them off as well. He'd paged her, but she hadn't responded. Actually he hadn't seen her much, since that day at the beach.

Was she finding it awkward to see him? Since he'd skipped his normal Monday ER visit this week, he would say she wasn't the only one.

As long as they didn't let it damage their working relationship beyond repair.

She suddenly appeared out of nowhere, her hands deep in the pockets of her pants.

"Sorry, I had a patient. I was afraid I was going to miss you."

She looked toward him, but not quite at him.

Well, that was fine.

Grace reached up and clasped Addy's hands. "Thank you so much for everything. I can't believe how amazingly lucky we were. Mom says the house is almost as good as new. After only a week."

"That's wonderful. And Matthew is doing okay?" This time she met his eyes as if seeking confirmation for her words.

He gave her a nod. "Yes, he's well on his way to a full recovery."

Kind of like Garret was. As difficult and uncomfortable as the aftermath of that kiss had been, maybe it actually had accomplished something. Maybe it was busy working behind the scenes, sawing through the first link in a chain that bound him to his past. If so, the ocean should carry warning labels for those who didn't really want to be free.

Or maybe he did.

And he could admit—at least to himself—

that kissing her had been a memorable experience. She had definitely tasted like salt.

His mouth went up in a half smile. She must have caught it, because her head tilted in question. He gave a quick shake of his head to indicate it was nothing.

Beverly dropped a kiss onto the baby's head and shifted his weight higher on her hip. "He's doing great. He's back to being as ornery as he ever was."

Right now, the baby looked anything but ornery as he smiled and babbled, staring at the lobby as if it was the most fascinating place he'd ever been. The bruising around his eyes was fading, a yellow shadow replacing the red and black he'd been sporting.

And his fracture should heal without any problems.

Something twisted inside Garret, obliterating his pleasant thoughts from a few minutes earlier. At least this family would get their happy ending.

Beverly was actually thinking of relocating to South Beach. The fire might be just the motivation she'd needed to move closer to her grandchildren and daughter.

Addy went over and picked Matthew's

chubby hands and clapped them together several times, smiling when the baby laughed. "He's back to being as cute as ever, if you ask me."

She looked completely at ease with the baby, the furrow between her brows disappearing, her face shining with what looked like joy.

Oh, how he remembered that feeling. Looking down at Leticia had made his heart swell with love. A complete and utter happiness that he'd thought nothing could take away.

How wrong he'd been.

He swallowed, as the moment between Addy and Matthew continued, and for a brief instant something flashed inside his skull, before he blanked it out, taking a step back.

"Oh, I almost forgot," Beverly said. "Is the auction open to the public? I picked up a brochure."

"It's open to anyone who would like to come." He somehow managed to keep his voice smooth and calm, hoping any evidence of the turbulence inside was well hidden. "We should have a complete list of auction items a week before the gala, if you want to come by and pick one up. They'll be here in the lobby."

"I'll do that, thank you." Then Beverly turned to her daughter. "I'm going out to bring the car around."

"It's okay, Mom. I can walk."

"Are you sure, honey?"

"I'm positive." Grace's eyes went to her baby and then skipped away, a quick look of fear crossing her face. "If you could just strap Matthew in his car seat for me. I don't think I can manage yet with my hands."

Although her hands were still red, Garret was pretty sure she could click a baby into his seat without too much difficulty. After all, she'd grabbed Addy's hands and held them without a single wince. He glanced at the other doctor and saw her frown. So, he wasn't the only one who'd noticed.

Grace stood and turned toward him. "Thank you for everything. With Matthew especially."

"That's what we're here for. You have those cards I gave you?"

He'd given her the numbers of the hospital crisis line and chaplain in case she needed to talk to someone about what she was going through. Something he should have done much sooner than he had after his daughter passed away.

"I do. I won't need them, though."

"Hang on to them, okay? Just to make me feel better." The last thing he wanted to do was ask someone from social services to check in on the family, but if push came to shove, he would. Hopefully, with her mother there, things would click back into a normal rhythm.

Kind of like he was hoping would happen with him and Addy. That their little incident would be forgotten or that they would at least stop avoiding each other.

"I will. Thank you again." With that, they walked outside and made their way into the parking lot, one of the younger kids turning to give them a wave. Garret waved back.

"What cards was she talking about?"

"I gave her the number for the hospital counselor in case she needed to talk."

"I'm glad." She pulled her stethoscope from around her neck, coiled it and stuck it in the pocket of her sweater. "I was a little worried about how she was going to cope once she got home. I'm glad her mom is here."

"I was thinking that very same thing." He paused, then decided to act on his earlier thoughts. It was time to move past the beach, at least for him. "Can I buy you a cup of coffee?"

"Uh-oh. Am I in trouble again?"

This time he allowed himself to fully smile. "No. I think I might be the one who's in trouble, and I want to make things right."

"You're not. In trouble, that is. If you're talking about the day at the beach, don't worry about it. It was fun. Let's just call what happened a minor hiccup."

He'd hardly call that kiss a "hiccup," but better that than turn it into a crisis that caused her to call it quits on the hospital. "It *was* fun. Coffee?"

"I don't actually drink coffee, but a cup of tea might be nice. I'm due a lunch break anyway."

"It's almost three o'clock."

This time she laughed. "That tone says it all. We've had a busy day in the ER. But don't worry—I've only put in one hour more than usual today. But I am ready to get off my feet for a while."

A few minutes later they were in the hospital cafeteria, and she had a steaming cup of Earl Grey tea between her hands. While he had her here, he decided to broach something that had been brought up by one of the auction committee members. It also provided a means to put things back on a solid footing between them. "Part of the reason I wanted to have coffee—or tea—with you is we need a few volunteers to help display the items that are being auctioned off. Are you interested?"

She blinked a time or two. "Helping with the auction? How?"

"Mostly just holding up the donations while the auctioneer describes them. If you can't, I'll certainly understand. I know it's short notice."

"It's not that."

"Worried that your ex might show up?"

"Let's just say I'd rather not hold up the set of pearls while they're being auctioned off."

"Understandable. We'll have a couple of people there rotating in and out, so we'll be able to assign them to someone else." He took a sip of coffee. "Oh, and just so you know, I bought a surfboard."

She set her cup down on the table. "You did what?"

He had no idea why he'd just admitted that. But it seemed important somehow. Maybe he just needed her to know that he wasn't a quitter. With their earlier discussion about his hand, he wondered if he'd come across that way, just resigning himself to life behind a desk. Maybe this was one way to show her. He could even offer to do a little more consulting in the neurology department.

Why was it suddenly so important, when he wouldn't have even thought of doing so two or three months ago? He wasn't sure—didn't even want to question his motives too closely.

"I actually liked surfing. And since there is no snow here on South Beach…"

"Not much, no." She reached across as if she was going to touch him. He even braced himself for contact, but she changed her trajectory at the last second, setting her hand flat on the table instead. "I'm so glad, Garret. It really is kind of addictive."

Like her?

Not where he wanted his thoughts heading right now.

"I can see that it might be. I need to do

some more practice on my— What is it called again?"

"Pop up. And you were already getting the hang of it. A few more trips into the surf and you'll be well on your way."

"I guess I should have asked about sharks when we were out there."

It had been hard to think about anything that didn't revolve around her, when they'd been on that beach. And watching her slim limbs as she'd demonstrated how to stand up and ride a wave hadn't left room for worrying about anything but himself.

"There's danger in everything. We just do whatever we can to minimize the risks."

Minimize the risks.

The only way to do that with Addy was to avoid her entirely, and he wasn't willing to do that. Even though he found himself hyper-aware of everything she did, from the way her fingers curved around her teacup to the way a tiny dimple zipped in and out of sight on the corner of her mouth as she talked. It was fascinating, and he found himself watching and waiting for its next appearance.

Not good, Garret.

He was supposed to be here scoping things

out, hoping that the patches of quicksand had dried up.

And if they hadn't?

"We weren't wearing wetsuits, so there's not much danger of looking like a tasty seal snack to them, right?"

"Even those who wear them don't have much trouble. There's an occasional bite, but very few fatalities. I've been surfing most of my life, and I still have all my limbs. Just pay attention to the surfing conditions. There are several apps you can use."

"Okay, I'll do that."

"Good. Now, as far as holding up the auction items, please tell me I don't have to dress up like a game-show host and suddenly become graceful and beautiful."

She already was both of those, but to say it would be the same as ignoring those surf conditions she'd just talked about. These were dangerous waters full of riptides and crosscurrents. One wrong move and—

"No, just wear whatever you normally would to the auction."

"Why am I remembering the words 'black tie'?"

"Because it is?"

She groaned. "Ugh. That's not my cup of tea at all. I'm a true tomboy at heart."

A tomboy who surfed and looked totally at home on the water. He liked that. A little too much.

"You've been here longer than I have. Are you telling me you've never gone to one of these events?"

"Um, I'm a tomboy? Remember? I tend to stick to the donating side of things."

He'd assumed she was going to the fundraiser or he never would have asked her to participate. "I'm sorry. I didn't realize you weren't planning to be there."

"It's okay. It's about time I went to one. It's easy to forget about all the efforts that go into keeping this hospital in operation."

"Are you sure?"

"I am. If you can take up surfing, I can certainly make an appearance at the auction." She smiled and took another sip of her tea. "It seems we're both moving a little bit beyond our comfort zones."

"It appears so. I'm not sure if that's a good thing or a bad thing."

"Oh, it's a good thing, Garret. A very good thing."

CHAPTER SIX

ADDY KNOCKED ON the door to his office, even though Garret had told her to just go in and lay the auction participation form on his desk.

Knocking one more time to be sure, she opened the door and tiptoed into his office, which was ridiculous. He wasn't here, so there was no need to be quiet. She would just drop the paper on his desk and leave.

Laying the signed sheet in the very center of his desk, she was amazed by how clean it was. Nothing was on it but a three-tray wire rack, a pencil cup, a lamp and three rubber spheres the size of tennis balls. Each one was a different color and had a ring at one end of it. That was odd. She'd never noticed those before. Stress balls?

If so, why three of them? He only had two

hands. Maybe they were something for the auction. She touched one, something about them striking a tone in her memory banks. Where had she seen these before?

She froze. She'd seen them down in physical therapy. Something in her throat caught as she realized these were not stress balls at all. They were exercise balls for the hand. The ring went over the middle finger to keep the ball from being dropped by someone with a poor grip.

She was pretty sure these hadn't been on his desk the last time she'd been in here. He must have forgotten to put them away. She picked one up, allowing the rubber to sit in the middle of her palm. It was heavier than she'd expected.

"Having fun?"

Oh, God. Her eyes closed.

What had she been thinking? This was something very private, and for her to have handled them…

She turned to face him.

"Sorry, I actually thought they were something for the auction until I—"

"Until you—?"

He wasn't going to help her wiggle her way

out of this. She was supposed to have come into his office, dropped that paper on his desk and then turned around and walked out. Instead, she'd given herself license to explore, something he hadn't invited her to do.

"Until I remembered where I'd seen something similar." Her chin tilted. "I didn't realize you were still working on strengthening your hand. I'm glad."

It was the truth.

"I don't know why I got them out. They've pretty much done all they're going to do."

She set the ball in her hand next to the others, while Garret went around and sat in his chair.

"Is that what you told your patients? 'Well, six months of therapy hasn't helped. You might as well give up.'"

"Try four years."

She swallowed. Somehow she hadn't realized it had been that long since his accident. But, of course, he'd been at the hospital for three years, so the timing sounded right.

She picked up the ball she'd discarded. "Why keep them at all, if you're so sure they can't help?"

An irritable shrug was her answer. "Maybe as a reminder."

"You know what I think?"

"Are you going to tell me either way?" A muscle in his cheek told her to tread carefully, but, unlike him, Addy tended to wear her heart on her sleeve.

She said what she thought. "I think there's still a part of you that wants to help patients. I saw it in your eyes when you looked at Matthew."

"Oh, so you can read my thoughts now, can you?"

"No, but I know how I would feel if I were in your position."

"Do you?" He laid both hands on top of his desk. One of them spread flat; it became one with the surface it was on. The other hand sat awkwardly in a half crouch. Garret pushed down hard with it, the knuckles whitening, lines of pain forming on his face.

"Stop it."

He let the tension out of the damaged fingers and they went back to the way they were. "You're not in my position, though, are you? So you can't know how I do or don't feel."

She'd made him angry. That hadn't been

her intent. Actually, she hadn't been going to say anything about the strengthening balls at all, except he'd caught her with one in her hand.

But, dammit, his life wasn't over, and for him to act as if it were was just—

Infuriating.

"You need to get a grip." She tossed the ball at him. He caught it with ease with his good hand. "In more ways than one. Use those. Maybe they won't make a difference in what you can or can't do, but they can keep you from losing the gains from whatever therapy you've had."

All the caged emotion seemed to drain out of him in an instant. "Maybe you do know after all."

"I don't, Garret." She went around the desk and touched his shoulder. "I truly don't. But don't settle for something less than what your heart wants."

"And if my heart wants something it can't have?"

She knew all about that. She'd give anything to talk to her mom one more time. And for her mom to recognize her as her daughter. But that wasn't going to happen. Garret wasn't faced with that kind of useless wishing. He could still salvage his situation into something good.

"Then find a compromise," she said. "Something that gives you purpose and meaning."

He stood and faced her. "You think I don't have that with my current job?"

"I don't know." She nodded toward the therapy balls. "I'm not trying to tell you what to do. You have to decide that for yourself."

He stared down at her for a long moment, a series of emotions moving across his face. Unexpectedly, he cupped her cheek, the warmth of his hand sifting into her system.

Shock held Addy completely still, her lungs filled with air she didn't dare release. He leaned down and brushed his lips across her cheek in the lightest of touches. Then he was gone, moving halfway across the room to where a leather sofa and two chunky chairs sat. He shoved his hands in his pockets. "Thank you, Addy. For believing in the impossible."

"Hey, you didn't think you could surf either." She smiled, although her system was still a wobbly mess over that kiss. A kiss that hadn't even touched her lips, but had moved her more deeply than the one on the beach. Because the beach kiss had come from a place of physical attraction. Lust, even. And this one? It had come from the heart.

She'd never had anything like that with Leo. They'd had the lust. They'd had what she'd thought was love. But moments like this had been absent.

And, boy, she'd better be careful about where she allowed this to carry her. Having a harmless crush was one thing. Letting it grow into anything deeper?

Well, that was something entirely different. The next time she got involved with a man, she wanted things to go slow. She wanted to take her time and make sure she got it right. Make sure she knew everything about her partner.

And Garret was still her boss. She had no business getting into a relationship—no, not a relationship, an *infatuation*-ship—with him.

"The jury is still out on the surfing. But I'm going to practice." He opened his palm to show the ball she'd tossed him a few seconds ago. He put it into his damaged hand and contracted his fingers.

He was going to practice more things than surfing. At least, she hoped that was what he meant by his actions.

A smile played on her lips. She was suddenly happy, and she wasn't sure why. But right now she didn't care. All that mattered was he wasn't giving up.

"I would ask for a high five, but I think that's part of what got us in trouble last time."

"Hmm, I disagree. I think it was the bikini."

She laughed. "I think it was the shirt."

"The shirt?"

"Well, let's just say it was the lack of a shirt."

He blinked, then gave a grin that went straight up her spine and lodged in the part of the brain that housed her emotions.

"Well, unless we want to get ourselves in trouble again, maybe we'd better confine our talk to something besides our clothes."

Her happiness turned into a sense of giddy euphoria. She should stop, just as he'd said, but she couldn't resist one last riposte.

"Ha, Dr. I-can't-take-the-heat-so-I'm-getting-out-of-the-kitchen Stapleton, I'll take that as my cue to leave."

He took a step forward and her eyes widened, but he didn't stop in front of her. He went to the door instead.

"Oh, I can take the heat just fine." Even as he said it, he twisted the knob and opened the door. "It's just not the right place. Or the right time."

She went out throwing him what she hoped was a saucy smile, even though, inside, her heart was shivering with a new kind of heat. Garret wanted her.

And, Lord help her, she wanted him too.

Just as Adelina was getting ready to head out for the night, her purse already slung over her shoulder, an elderly woman hobbled into the emergency room, using a walker. Glancing past her, Addy looked for whoever had brought her in, but there was no one, unless that person was parking the car.

They'd had a few people trickle in this evening, but it hadn't been enough to take her mind off what had happened in Garret's office.

He was going to keep trying? Because of what she'd said?

She was giving herself way too much credit.

"Can I help you?"

"I need a doctor."

Addy prayed Garret was already gone and wouldn't come down here. "I'm a doctor. What seems to be the problem?"

"It's not for me. It's for my husband."

She again glanced toward the door. "Is he in the car?" She didn't see how the woman could have driven a vehicle. She was barely able to keep herself upright. That was when she realized the woman was wearing a stained bathrobe rather than street clothes.

"Can't you see him? He's right here."

She swallowed. "What's your name?"

"He's right here. You're just not looking hard enough. His name is Daniel Lloyd Trentford. And I'm Marilyn Trentford."

A nurse came through the doors. She looked at Addy in open puzzlement.

"Can you look up a chart for me? Marilyn Trentford."

"Right away."

The woman gave her walker a little thump

against the floor. "It's not for me, I told you. It's for my husband. He's ill."

Addy nodded and motioned Marilyn to follow her. "Let's take him back to an exam room, then, shall we?"

Waiting patiently as the woman made her way into the back, she intercepted the nurse, who spoke in low tones. "I overheard part of your conversation. I looked up her chart, and she does have a husband. But his name is Ben, not Daniel." There was a moment's hesitation. "Marilyn was diagnosed with Alzheimer's three years ago."

Addy's fingers curled into her palm as a spear of pain arced through her.

"You're sure."

"I am, sorry."

She might actually need Garret's help for this one, if he was still here. "Can you see if Dr. Stapleton is in his office, while I get Mrs. Trentford into a room? And call the number she has listed and see who answers the phone." She was afraid if she said Ben's name, the woman might grow agitated.

Once she was in a room, she proceeded to get vitals on Marilyn, even though she protested that she wasn't the one who needed a doctor. Everything seemed normal, although her blood pressure was a little low. Addy also wanted to check for a urinary tract infection, since that could cause confusion in some elderly patients. If she had Alzheimer's, though, that was probably the cause of what basically amounted to a hallucination.

Garret came into the room a minute later with a frown directed right at her.

"Before you say anything, I was headed out the door. There's my purse."

"Good to know." He glanced at the patient. "Neuro consult?"

"No, I need some advice. Can I see you outside for a minute?"

Once they were in the hallway, she gave him a quick rundown of what they were dealing with. "In short, Ann is calling the house to see if her husband—her *real* husband—is home."

"And if he's not?"

"That's where I need the advice. Do I call social services?"

"We may have to, if we can't find a caregiver."

Ann came over a minute later. "I got an answer at the house."

"And?" Addy and Garret responded at the same time.

"Mrs. Trentford's son is there, but I'm afraid— Well, he found Mr. Trentford dead of what looks like natural causes. And when he went to look for his mother, he couldn't find her anywhere. He's relieved she's safe."

Tears blurred Addy's eyes for a moment. "She walked all the way to the hospital, and no one noticed?"

It was now pitch black outside and the streets of South Beach were no doubt gearing up for another Friday night of partying. It was a wonder she hadn't been hit by a car at some point.

Ann gave her shoulder a quick squeeze. "She knew enough to try to get help for him, even if she couldn't remember his name."

"How did she even find the hospital?"

"She's been here quite a bit. It could just be imprinted somehow. Who knows? Alzheimer's doesn't always follow a prescribed course."

Garret glanced at the closed door, his jaw tight. "Is her son coming for her?"

"He's waiting on the coroner to get to the

house for his dad. But his sister—Mrs. Trentford's daughter—is on her way."

Addy knew this scenario played out time and time again across the nation, but it never failed to break her heart when someone came in with dementia. Her mom had passed away from it in this very hospital a year ago. Ann would remember that, which was why she'd squeezed her shoulder.

And tomorrow was her mom's birthday. She was going to put flowers on her grave—the start of what she hoped would become a yearly tradition. Her mom had loved daisies, her flower beds had been filled with them, until she could no longer remember how to care for them.

Garret didn't know any of that, however. And there was no reason to tell him.

"I'll just go make her comfortable, until they get here."

When she turned to go to the room, though, Garret stopped her. "Are you okay? You seem a little funny."

"I'm fine."

It was a lie, but he wouldn't know that. Unless he could somehow see the hard squeeze of her heart in her chest.

"You don't look fine. Why don't you let me take this one?"

"I want to care for her."

Ann stepped in. "I'll do it, Dr. Santini. Why don't you go ahead on home? Her daughter will be here soon."

She stood there, torn. There was really nothing she could do. And she could still remember her dad's heartbreak over her mom's death as if it were yesterday. Even though her mom hadn't known any of them by the time she passed away, he'd still insisted on caring for her every moment of the day. Then she'd choked on some food and contracted aspiration pneumonia.

Her dad was still living on his own in the house where Addy was raised, and, although she grieved her mother's death, she was glad her father was no longer shouldering that weight by himself.

Would Marilyn even realize her husband was gone?

That wasn't any of her business. "Thanks, Ann. I do appreciate it."

"Sure thing. Go home."

She went back in the room to retrieve her

handbag. "Ann, one of our nurses, is going to come in and help you get settled."

"What about Daniel?"

Addy swallowed hard. "She'll help him too."

Then, feeling like the worst form of traitor, she walked out of the room and started down the hallway. Garret fell in step beside her.

"I think I need a drink," she said.

"May I ask why?" He tugged her arm to make her stop walking. "And if you're planning on driving home afterward?"

"I'll catch a cab—don't worry."

"How about if I join you?"

"Why?"

"Let's just say I've had a rough day as well." He rolled his eyes. "Hospital politics. Nothing new."

She hadn't told him about her mom, but he seemed to sense something was wrong.

"Are you going to take a taxi as well?"

"I'll be the designated driver." He smiled. "I don't generally drink anymore. But if you're planning on getting completely wasted, you might want to give me your address before you're too far gone."

"Nope. One drink is my limit. But I would

appreciate the ride home. I'll catch a cab to work and pick up my car tomorrow. It'll be safe in the parking lot."

A half hour later, they were in one of the bars that didn't boast thumping music or a party atmosphere, because Addy was definitely not in the mood for a party of any type. Instead it was a small Irish pub that served sandwiches with their liquor. Addy had been planning to get a margarita, but decided on a dark ale instead.

"A surfer with a penchant for dark bitter beer."

The grief that had threatened to overcome her in the hospital dissipated. "I have to keep people on their toes."

"I'd say you do that on a regular basis."

The waiter brought their drinks and took their food order. Garret was getting a burger, medium rare, while she was getting a turkey club. "A doctor who eats partially cooked meat. What would our patients say?"

"I deal with politics, nowadays, not patients, remember? So I'm pretty sure they wouldn't care."

Damn, she'd forgotten that he didn't practice anymore. Garret still had all the mannerisms of a doctor. "You treated Matthew. And I'm sure there are others you've looked after since your accident."

He took a long drink of his water. "Nope. Matthew was the first."

"He's the first patient you've treated in four years?"

"Yes."

She couldn't help but wonder if he was headed down a wrong path. Whether he could operate or not, he should be in there consulting or diagnosing, something where he could still have a hand in medicine, even with a damaged hand. But that was his choice. She'd already tried to meddle once and he'd rebuffed her in no uncertain terms.

"Well, you did a great job. I'm pretty sure his mother thought so as well."

"There was no choice and no one else. It was as simple as that." He leaned forward. "Mind telling me what that little exchange between you and Ann was back at the hospital, and why you suddenly felt the need to come to a bar?"

She toyed with how much to share, but decided to hell with it. Why shouldn't he know? Maybe he already did, in fact.

"My mom died of Alzheimer's a year ago. It was a long hard road. And her birthday is tomorrow."

"I'm sorry. Tonight's situation with Marilyn must have hit hard. Your dad?"

"He's still alive and well, but it was an awful time for him—for all of us. She lived for five and a half years after her diagnosis. But at least she wasn't aware of what was happening at the end."

It hadn't helped that Leo had pretty much withdrawn from the marriage by the time she died. It made the grieving process that much harder. He attended the funeral, but as far as emotional support? There'd been nothing. So it shouldn't have come as much of a shock that he'd cheated. She hadn't exactly been a fun partner for the last couple of years. She wasn't going to tell Garret any of that, though.

"Any siblings to help you through?"

"Nope. I was an only child and my mom was my rock. And that rock slowly rolled further and further away, until it was a mere speck on the horizon. And then one day it blipped out of sight forever."

"It's a pretty terrible disease."

"Yes, it is. And when she was first diagnosed, I kind of went crazy. Made some stupid choices. Got married." She took a deep drink of her beer, welcoming the bitter taste that lingered at the back of her tongue.

"Ouch. But I do understand about making stupid choices."

She swallowed her mouthful of brew. "What about your parents? Still living?"

"Yes. They're in New York. Both retired at this point. My dad was a neurosurgeon like—like I was. My mom was a schoolteacher. She still tutors algebra on the side."

"Algebra. Wow. That's impressive." And his parents were probably the same age as hers. He was blessed to have them both alive and healthy. "Do *you* have any sisters or brothers?"

"I have a younger sister. She's a colonel in the army."

"You have very strong family members."

"Yes. Your dad had to have been pretty strong too, from what you just said."

He was, and that was what had made her life with Leo such a disappointment. He'd presented himself as calm and stable, something she'd really needed at the time, but the reality had been far from that. He'd barely scraped by in his studies to be an EMT. And wanting to get divorce counseling?

She pushed her beer away from her with a suddenness that almost sloshed some of the liquid over the rim of the glass.

"Are you okay?"

"I must be a lighter weight than I thought."

If he suspected she wasn't quite telling the truth he didn't say anything. And then the waiter had their food ready, placing the plates in front of them and asking if there was anything else they wanted.

"I think we're good," Garret said.

"Thanks for coming with me. You were right. That patient hit me a little harder than I realized."

"It saved me from going home to an empty house. It's nice to go places from time to time. Something I haven't done in a while."

"Me either." She and Leo hadn't gone anywhere together since her mother died. There was no way their marriage could have survived, affair or no affair.

They ate their food, the conversation turning to lighter subjects like medical school horror stories. They'd gone to different schools but the trials and tribulations were the same everywhere, it seemed. Every school had "that" instructor. One who seemed to delight in making students' lives miserable.

"You'd never be that guy," she told Garret. She pulled up short, realizing what she'd just said. "Sorry."

"It's okay. I'm not saying I'll never teach, but it's not on my radar at the moment. My current job keeps me pretty busy."

Well, at least he was no longer reciting that stupid quote about teachers not being able to do what they taught.

He went on. "Are you that anxious to get rid of me?"

"What? Of course not."

He smiled. "Maybe you have your eye on my job."

"Huh-uh. No way. You couldn't pay me enough to be a hospital administrator."

"Why not?"

She pulled her glass back toward her, deciding maybe she did need a little more after all. It seemed she was determined to keep stepping into dangerous territory. The beer would either set her on a right path or make it so that she didn't care if she stumbled into a ravine. Too bad Garret wasn't indulging as well. Then maybe he wouldn't remember every stupid word she was busy spitting out.

"It just isn't something I'd be interested in. Your mom is good at algebra. I am not."

"I don't remember using any algebra at all in my job."

Do not use the term "bean counter," Addy, if you know what's good for you.

"Since I don't really know what your job involves, I guess I shouldn't make blanket statements like that. I'm just not an administrator type. I'd rather be out on the floor doing stuff."

Another gulp of the bitter brew to wash her mouth out. She was such an idiot. Maybe she really was a lightweight and the beer was doing the talking. Somehow she didn't think so, though.

This time Garret didn't correct her or tell her she was wrong about his job.

"I'd rather be out on the floor 'doing stuff' too. But since I can't—"

And that was so much worse. Because he'd put her in her place with a plop and there wasn't a damned thing she could do about it. Because he was right. Hospital administrator wasn't his chosen profession. He was a surgeon. Except surgery was now out of his reach.

It was really none of her business what he did, or what field he chose to go into. Sometimes life dealt you a bad hand. And sometimes you dealt yourself a bad hand. He'd had an accident after falling asleep at the wheel. And Addy had married a man who was wrong for her in so many ways. They'd both whipped up disasters and been forced to dine at the table afterward no matter how awful the main course turned out to be.

But, as he'd said at the beach, you could learn from your mistakes and avoid making them again.

She was never going to jump into a relationship without carefully considering the person and the timing. She and Leo had come together and married way too quickly. The fact that disappointment had come just as quickly shouldn't have been a surprise to either of them.

"You're right, Garret. And this is why I shouldn't drink. And why I should have come by myself. I hope you'll forgive anything I've said that might be off the mark."

He smiled. "Was it really the beer talking? I seem to remember having some of these same conversations and you were stone-cold sober at the time."

She laughed. "Okay, you've got me there. My mouth has gotten me in trouble plenty of times—as you can tell. I remember more than one teacher sending home a note to my parents with that same remark. I'll try to do better."

"I like that you say what you think. So many people don't anymore."

The topic changed to treatment options and work-related subjects and Addy was off the hook. Because these were things they could agree or disagree on without being in danger of stepping on each other's toes. She assumed Garret was divorced. He'd never actually mentioned a wife, but had said his daughter died of leukemia. So either he'd been a single dad or he was divorced or separated.

And then they were done with their meal and Garret was asking if she wanted to walk down the sidewalk on this balmy South Beach evening.

She did, and she wasn't sure why, other than she'd enjoyed tonight far more than she should have. Maybe it was just such a change from what she'd had with Leo.

The moon was huge as they strolled down the walkway, its reflection on the ocean turning it into a shimmery curtain. She'd come out here a few times with friends when she was younger, and they'd actually skinny-dipped at midnight without anyone catching them. Another of the times she'd let her impulsiveness take charge.

Not that she was going to skinny-dip with Garret.

So why did she itch to go down to the shore and feel the sand between her toes? Because it was a beautiful night, and she didn't often get down this way anymore after dark.

"Do you think we could walk on the beach before we leave?"

"I'm not exactly dressed for wading."

He wasn't. His polo shirt and chinos were very business-oriented. But that didn't matter. She'd already told herself she wasn't going to do anything wild and crazy. So they'd be fine.

"Neither am I. It's just so gorgeous, and we're right here." She turned to face him, walking backward, the breeze lifting her hair off her neck and making her sigh. "Come on. Just for a few minutes."

"You talked me into it."

"Good."

Kicking off the low heels she'd worn to work, she twisted the side of her loose gauzy skirt into a knot that held it up without actually revealing anything more than a little sliver of her legs. She bent down to pick up her shoes and then ventured onto the fine grains that made up the beach. The sand was still warm from the afternoon sun and felt so good against her bare toes. She glanced back to make sure Garret was following her lead.

He was. He'd taken off his shoes and socks and had rolled his pants up to midcalf. His legs were still tanned from their outing last week.

Her mouth watered.

The man looked as good in business attire as he did in his board shorts. It wasn't fair. He had everything a woman could possibly want in the looks department. And the more she learned about him, the more she realized he had a lot going for him in the personality department as well. She held her arms out from her sides and closed her eyes, letting the breeze flow across her. Her skirt billowed against her legs, a sensual tickle that nothing could imitate.

"Feels so good out here."

"Yes, it does." The words were a soft murmur. "I don't think I've ever walked on a beach at night."

Her eyes flew open. "You're kidding."

"I didn't grow up in a coastal town, remember? I went for walks in Central Park instead."

"Is it as beautiful as this?" Her arms were still outstretched, and she did a slow spin to encompass everything around them: the sand, the moon, the stars glistening on the water.

"There are a lot of beautiful things in this world."

Something about the slow solemn way he said that made her stop turning, a shiver going over her. He was watching her, hands planted low on his hips, his bad one seeming to perch comfortably for once. His shoes were now on the ground beside him. "Addy…"

"Yes?" Her breath caught in her throat.

He took a step closer. "I think I'm about to do something incredibly stupid."

"I doubt that." And if the look on his face was any indication, she was in complete agreement.

"Just how drunk are you?"

"Am I acting like I am? I didn't even drink the whole beer. I'm just so glad to be out here tonight…" She hesitated, then decided to just say it. "With you."

"I was hoping you'd say that."

In a second, he had closed the gap between them, his right hand encircling her wrist and tugging her to him.

And when his head came down, she knew the kiss was coming. Only this time, it would be different than the previous one. Very, very different.

CHAPTER SEVEN

ADDY'S HOUSE WAS the closest, and the second she unlocked the door, they were through it, the passion that had ignited on the beach still burning just as strong after the ten-minute drive—which had seemed to take forever. The only saving grace were the kisses that punctuated the stoplights along the way.

Somehow he managed to close the front door and then his mouth found hers again. The taste of beer still clung to her lips along with whatever it was that made Addy, Addy.

She was intoxicating. Breathtaking. More heady than any alcohol known to man. And tonight, he planned to drink his fill. It seemed as if the last couple of weeks had been leading to this very place, and, right now, Garret couldn't think of anywhere he'd rather be.

Her arms twined around his neck, body

flattening to his, and, heaven help him, his libido was already roaring at him to pick up the pace.

No way. No how.

If they ended up in bed—and he hoped to hell they did—he wanted this to last for as long as possible.

He'd told himself to stay away from her after that surfing lesson, but they were both adults. This didn't have to go any further than one night of wild sex. If she was using him to drown out the pain of losing her mom, even better. Neither one of them needed a permanent relationship. She was in the midst of getting a divorce and he was in the throes of…

He had no idea. All he knew was he wasn't getting married again. Or having kids.

His good hand slid beneath the back of her shirt, the warmth and softness of her skin making something growl to life inside him. No, it wasn't just growling to life. It was already wide awake and howling for attention.

Addy's palms cupped the back of his head, one on either side of his neck. She leaned back slightly as her lips left his.

"Where?"

He knew exactly what she was asking.

"Babe, it's your house. You choose."

The endearment had dropped from his tongue without warning, and he tensed for a second. But if she minded, he couldn't tell. Right now, her thumbs were drawing designs in his hair that were getting to him in all the right places.

She glanced toward the back of the house and her teeth came down on her lower lip as if puzzling through something or other. "How about the couch? It's long and… It's long."

"It can be the floor, for all I care."

She leaned up and whispered in his ear, her warm breath slicing and dicing his control. "The floor would be *much* too uncomfortable."

"The couch it is, then."

Her hands slid down his back, fingers tucking into the waistband of his pants, sending another jolt of need through him.

He took a long, slow drink of her mouth, before murmuring, "Lead the way."

Taking him by the hand, she tugged him through a door that opened to the dining room, a big round table giving him some definite ideas, before she ducked through yet another doorway.

The living room.

And she was right. The couch was long. And it went in two directions, forming an L. It was perfect.

Just as she was.

His index finger touched her bottom lip then glided over her chin and slid over her throat, reaching the rounded neckline of her stretchy top.

God, he wished he had a second hand. Or at least one that worked. He didn't try to un-button the front; instead he let his palm wander down, bumping over her breast, hearing her hiss of air as he did. "Will this go over your head?"

She didn't ask what he meant, just took the initiative and made short work of the buttons. "They can be tricky."

They weren't, but he blessed her for sparing him the ordeal of having to fumble with them. He could do it, he did up his own shirts daily, but it took a while. Doing it for some-one else would embarrass him somehow, even though it was a ridiculous feeling. And nowadays, he tended to wear polos instead of shirts with a long line of buttons unless it was a special occasion.

She let her blouse drop to the ground and stood there in her skirt and a very lacy white bra that played peekaboo with his gaze. For a few seconds he couldn't do anything other than stare.

"You're beautiful, Addy."

She smiled. "You're pretty nice yourself." Moving forward, she kissed the bottom of his throat, her tongue swirling in the spot at the base of it. Then she reached behind him and balled up the bottom of his shirt and tugged it out of his pants and tried to pull it over his head. He bent forward slightly to help her. Then it was on the ground beside hers.

With one arm around her waist, he walked her backward until her legs met the couch. She sat and kicked her shoes off, then lay back. He followed her down, sliding up her body, using his elbows and hands to support his torso. "You're right. Comfortable couch. I approve."

"Yes, it is." She leaned up to lick along his lower lip. "And it's still a virgin."

He blinked for a second before smiling. "You and your—?"

"No. Never."

"Ah…in that case." His good hand slid behind her back and felt for the clasp on her bra. Found it. Snapped it open and then pulled the lacy item off from the front. He tossed it over the side of the couch.

He swallowed, awed and a little uncertain with how this was going to work. He hadn't been with a woman since his divorce.

Oh, he knew the mechanics, and that he could get there, but he wanted more than that. He wanted her to enjoy it. Wanted to take her to heights she'd never reached before.

Only he wasn't sure he could.

As if she sensed his doubts, she ran her hands up his back and tickled behind his ear. "Roll over, Garret."

"What?"

"You heard me."

She half hefted him when he didn't move fast enough, but then he was on his back, with her half sprawled across him. Tucking her skirt up around her upper thighs, she sat up and straddled his hips. And there was no way she could miss his reaction to her. Not quite the way he'd envisioned this going, but he appreciated her removing some of the worry more than she could know.

"So, now that I've lured you into my lair," she whispered, "what should I do with you?"

She had a skirt on. No buttons. No zipper. That was a good start. As were those creamy breasts that jiggled with every move she made.

"You should lean down here so I can kiss you."

Right on cue, she curved her torso forward, only he didn't kiss her mouth. Lowering his head, he sought out the curve of her breast, using his hand to cup it and help him reach. And reach he did. When his tongue stroked across her nipple she whimpered, back arching into him.

He took that as a sign and settled in to enjoy.

She planted her hands on his shoulders and balanced, her hips pressing down and hitting him in just the right spot.

It was ecstasy. And torture.

Time to somehow get that condom he carried out of his wallet. He'd kept one there, but had never used it. And right now he wasn't sure how he was going to get it on. One-handed it would have to be.

Letting go of her, he shoved his hand under himself and found his back pocket and the wallet in it. He grappled it out and flipped it open. Most of the time, he laid it on a counter and pulled whatever he needed from it, but right now, he was upside down and had no flat surface in sight. And there was no way he was going to hold it in his teeth.

Without hesitation, Addy took it from him. "Where?"

"There's a compartment in the side of—"

"Found it." She fiddled with the opening and then pulled the packet out and got to her feet. "You take care of what you need to, and I'll take care of what I need to." She set the wallet on an end table and laid the condom on his stomach. Then she reached under her skirt and down came her panties.

Garret's heart began pumping out obscenities in his chest. The very best kind.

Right. He was supposed to be doing something. He undid his button and zipper and pushed his pants and briefs down his hips. His shoes were already gone, so Addy tugged his socks free one by one. Then she took hold of his trousers and pulled them the rest of the way off along with his underwear until he was bare before her.

She licked her lips, taking the condom package and ripping it open.

"I can do it."

"Okay." She handed it to him and watched him roll it down his length, her eyes focused on the act.

So much for taking his time. He wanted her. Badly. And he knew himself well enough to realize he wasn't going to last. "Come here."

"I thought you'd never ask." Straddling him once again, she cupped his face and kissed him, the contact sweet and hot and everything in between. "Mmm, hurry."

"Hell, I don't want to—"

"It's okay. It'll be good. I've wanted this."

She had? Well, so had he. More than he cared to admit.

Grasping a hold of himself, he brushed over her, gently, feeling his way. Any ideas he might have had about entering her slowly went to hell. The second he was in position she took his entire length with one hard push.

He swore. And prayed. Broke out in a cold

sweat as he willed himself to hold very, very still.

She moved, but when he tried to stop her, she ignored him.

Taking his hand, she pressed it to her. "Go, Garret. Oh, go!"

Finding her, he stroked and squeezed while she rode him, her head thrown back, hair tumbling loose around her shoulders. She moaned, lips parted as she held herself steady with one hand on the back of the couch and continued to rise and fall.

And then he felt it. Boiling up inside him in an uncontrollable tide. He gritted his teeth as it poured over him, aware on some level that she was climaxing as well, her body contracting around his and urging him to lose himself inside her.

Minutes passed. His eyes had closed at some point. And she'd stopped moving. He reached up and curved an arm around her back, hauling her down to him, kissing her bare shoulder.

"That was…"

Her breath came out in a long hum of sound. "Yes, it was."

She settled against him, nuzzling closer

to his chest, head turned sideways. Her hair tickled his chin, but he didn't care. A slow contentment began to weave its way through him. He didn't want her to get up. Didn't want to ever move off this couch.

But maybe she wanted him out, now that it was over.

When his hand moved, though, she murmured, "No. Stay. Please."

He was pretty sure that tomorrow he was going to feel differently about spending the night, but right now…? Right now he was perfectly happy to stuff any and all doubts about what they'd done out of sight and worry about them later. Because he was going to do exactly what she asked. He was going to stay with her. All night long.

Addy covered him with the sheet she'd taken from the linen closet. He didn't stir. Waking up and seeing his face all soft with sleep, that injured hand for once out in plain sight… She gulped as a wave of longing swept over her.

When he'd asked where she wanted to make love, she'd frozen for a second or two. She hadn't wanted to go to her bed, didn't sleep in it herself, much less want to spend the night there with another man. She'd been meaning to toss it out and get a new one, but she just hadn't had the time to go and look for one.

The couch had seemed like the perfect spot.

And it had been. It still was. He looked gorgeous parked there, his clothes now neatly folded over one of the arms.

His insecurities over how to proceed had been obvious and had touched her deeply. There had been no need to worry, however. It had been fantastic. Better than she could have imagined.

She shivered, realizing she wanted him all over again.

Lord, it probably shouldn't have happened.

She'd slept with him for all the wrong reasons: the Alzheimer's patient had set off a fresh round of grief about losing her mom. She hadn't wanted to be alone.

She was having a hard time caring about the should-not-haves. They were adults. And it was good sex. Very good sex, since she was standing there contemplating waking him up for some more of the same. People here did things like this all the time and never thought a thing of it.

Easy to think that now. But what she'd do when he actually got up, she had no idea.

For now, she could go cook some breakfast.

She heated the skillet and then cracked some eggs, flipping them with a flick of her wrist a few minutes later. Between that and the smell of the bacon she'd started in another pan, she had to admit, she was famished.

Hopefully when he woke up it wouldn't turn all awkward and complicated.

Why wouldn't it?

She'd been issuing orders right and left last night. "Roll over. Hurry."

Yikes. She'd never realized she had the heart of a drill sergeant. She didn't. She'd simply been trying to ease the way for him, never stopping to think that maybe he would find that uncomfortable.

He would have said something if it was. Wouldn't he?

Her own doubts began crowding in, making her second-guess everything she'd done.

"No fair."

She whirled around and found him with

his pants back on his hips, the zipper still undone. And his briefs? Nowhere to be seen that she could tell.

"What do you mean?"

He took several steps into the room. "You're up. And dressed."

She'd had that same thought a few minutes earlier.

"Shouldn't I be? It's six o'clock."

"On Saturday. Do you work one of the shifts today?"

"Not until noon." She grinned, turning off the burner controls. "But I have something I need to do this morning."

He grabbed her around the waist and yanked her to him. "So do I." His head was just lowering to kiss her when a piece of bacon made a loud popping sound.

They laughed. And broke apart so she could turn off the other burner.

"What was it you had to do?" he asked as he stood behind her, watching.

She hesitated. "I want to put flowers on my mom's grave for her birthday. She loved daisies, and I think she would like knowing someone thought about her today." A rush of tears formed, and she struggled to push them back. "I hope she knew how much my dad and I loved her."

"Daisies." Something about his voice made her swipe at her eyes and then whirl around to look at him. What she saw shocked her.

He had his good hand braced on the countertop, holding himself upright, while a muscle worked in his jaw. Tight lines radiated out from his eyes.

He looked like a man in agony.

"What is it? Your hand?" Her glance went down to his side, where his injured fingers were curled in their normal position.

"No. It's not my hand." He stopped, then shook his head. "I should go."

He pulled up his zipper and fumbled with the button on his pants.

And just like that, the mood was gone. No more fuzzy feelings. No more playful words.

Just Garret's face, which looked—blank.

He'd seemed fine a few minutes ago. Maybe the pop of the bacon had jerked him back to his senses.

Ugh. What was she thinking, begging him to stay until morning and then tucking him in and cooking him a cozy breakfast?

They weren't friends. Or really even colleagues.

He probably thought she was a complete idiot. God, how stupid could she be?

It didn't stop her from trying to salvage the situation, though. "Do you want something to eat before you go?"

"No, I'll grab a bite a little later. Thanks, though." He went into the other room and when he came back he was completely dressed, including his socks and shoes.

"I guess I'll see you at work on Monday."

"Yes." He walked to the door, leaving her to follow him. "And, Addy?"

"Yes?" Why did she suddenly feel as if she could burst into tears at any minute?

"I'm sure your mom knew you loved her very much."

And with those quiet words, he let himself out of the door and closed it with a quiet click.

He'd signed the divorce papers. She'd tossed the packet on her console by the door. The day of their argument in front of the ER, he'd said he wanted to do divorce counseling before signing anything. She'd been flabbergasted. He had cheated on her. Was now living with his girlfriend. And he was worried about an amicable split?

He'd evidently changed his mind about the counseling. The thick envelope from his lawyer had been in her mailbox when she'd come home from work last night.

A week had passed since she'd placed flowers on her mom's grave, since Garret had walked away from her house after uttering a line that had made her sink to the ground and cry the second the door had closed behind him.

She'd barely seen him since then, and the regrets she hadn't had the night they had sex had been growing like weeds ever since. Now they were tall and thick and choked out anything that might have disagreed.

What had you pictured, Addy? A kiss on the cheek as he sent you off to work?

Maybe she'd expected a series of cozy little rendezvous with Garret. Well, that was not going to happen.

Thank God he'd used protection. For both of their sakes. The last thing she needed was to get pregnant by accident. Leo had wanted to wait a while before having kids. That "while" had turned into their entire marriage.

She should have seen it for the sign that it was.

And now she was thirty-five and wondering if it was too late and feeling like a fool. In more ways than one.

Well, she could consider this her free pass, redeemable for one dumb move.

And which move was that? Marrying Leo? Or having sex with Garret?

Well, if Garret hadn't taken off like a shot, she might have considered that a casual dalliance. People did it all the time, right?

Just because she wasn't built like that, didn't mean there was anything wrong with it.

How about the fact that Garret seemed to be avoiding her like the plague?

Maybe she needed to confront him and clear the air. He hadn't exactly apologized, but the way he'd left had bothered her.

Whatever it was, they couldn't go on avoiding each other forever. Besides, they were down to a week and a half before the auction. She and the other volunteers were supposed to meet with him and some of the marketing team this morning to discuss everyone's part in it. She was going to see him. Unless she dropped out of helping.

She thought for a second.

No. She'd given her word. He might be uncomfortable about what had happened, but that didn't mean she was going to change her life over it. Besides, he was the one who'd asked her to participate in the fund-raiser, so he could just suck it up and deal with it.

And afterward? She was going to corner him and either figure this out or agree not to figure it out. But she wasn't going to be made to feel she needed to duck for cover any time he was around.

With that decided, she headed off to the bedroom to take a shower and get dressed.

For work.

CHAPTER EIGHT

HE HAD A pretty good idea why Addy wanted to see him after the meeting. But the last thing he wanted to talk about was what had happened between them.

Her mention of putting flowers on her mom's grave had been a punch to the gut, reminding him that he'd avoided going to the cemetery for far too long. He and Patrice had gone together to put flowers on Leticia's grave for the first year after her death. Then he'd somehow had to work, whenever his wife had suggested it, so she'd gone alone. Continued to go alone. Until the accident. And then he'd moved here.

He should have been there. Should have gone to put flowers on his own child's grave, dammit!

His jaw clenched as he tried to rein in the emotions that were threatening to explode.

Addy had reminded him of everything he'd lost. And now she wanted to talk.

What the hell was there to say?

He had no idea, but right now, he needed to concentrate on getting through this meeting in one piece.

They were to the question-and-answer portion, and thank heavens this was Marketing's area. He'd been all too aware of Addy sitting out there in her scrubs, the lanyard around her neck proclaiming her a doctor of Miami's Grace Hospital.

And he was up here with the people who took care of the building and employees—but not patients.

"Last thing. We'd like to have a screen as in previous years that flashes through some of our hospital's success stories, so if you have any suggestions, please see me afterward so we can contact those patients and ask for a picture or two. We don't need details, since we have HIPAA laws to consider." Someone whispered something to the speaker. "Okay, I've just been told we've had some photographers floating around the hospital taking candids these past couple of weeks, so we'll intersperse your suggestions with those shots."

Garret leaned a shoulder against the wall, crossing his arms and scanning the twenty people in the room. When he got to Addy, she averted her eyes.

She'd been looking right at him.

That made him swallow. He'd walked away from her house without an explanation, without even eating the breakfast she'd obviously made for him.

And when he'd awoken, he'd found a sheet over him. That had turned him to warm mush. He'd gone to the kitchen intent on dragging her back to bed, and then she'd mentioned her mom's grave. About wondering if she knew she was loved. It was as if she'd dumped an icy bucket of water over him. All he'd wanted to do was get out of there.

Had Leticia known? Could she somehow see that he couldn't be bothered to go and visit her grave?

The meeting was over, but instead of coming over to talk to him, she went up to the front to talk to one of the presenters, instead.

He gave her a piece of paper and she scribbled something on it and then handed it back to him.

What was that all about?

A second later, she headed his way and his whole body tensed. Here it came.

"Can we go to your office, maybe?"

That made it official. Whatever she wanted to talk about was something she didn't want anyone to overhear.

"Sure." He tilted his head to indicate the table where the marketing person was still standing answering questions. "What was that about?"

"They asked for suggestions about the slideshow. I decided to give them Grace Turner's name."

"Grace…" His head cocked as something jogged his memory. "The house-fire family?"

"Yes. I thought they'd be a great choice."

"They would." He'd wondered a couple of times how that family was doing. Hopefully Grace was feeling better and had made her peace with what had happened.

He led the way to his office, which thankfully was just down the hallway from the meeting room. He started toward the desk and then changed his mind when he saw the exercise balls still sitting on top of it. He didn't want to pave the way for any more lectures on her part. Especially since he'd just stood in that meeting and wished he were sitting in one of the chairs instead of standing up at the front.

Motioning her to the sofa, he chose one of the chairs and then waited for whatever it was she had to say.

"So…" She leaned forward and clasped her hands on her knees. "I'm not sure exactly how to say this, but things have been awkward since— Well, you know. I'm not quite sure how to fix it."

"There's nothing to fix." That came out a little bit harsher than he'd meant for it to, so he tried again. "We work together. A relationship of any kind between us would be hard."

Her brows went up. "You think that's what this is about? That I want something more than what happened? Um, no. I'm in the middle of a divorce and I was mourning my mom. The last thing I want is to start something." Her face hardened. "Is that why you left so suddenly, and why you seem to be going out of your way to steer clear of me now? If so, don't worry. What happened was a onetime thing."

Despite her words, a flash of something that could have been hurt appeared in her eyes. He owed it to her to tell her the truth.

"I left like I did because I can't—didn't—put flowers on my daughter's grave."

"What?"

"You heard me."

"I did, but I don't understand. What does that have to do with what happened?"

"You mentioned getting flowers for your mom's grave and it brought back things I thought I'd dealt with. Evidently I haven't." He swallowed. "I didn't put flowers on Leticia's grave, even when I could. Even when I was still in New York. Her death did something to me. It changed me, and not for the better."

"I had no idea. I'm sorry."

"I didn't want to explain that morning. Didn't think I could get through an explanation, actually. So if you think I've been avoiding you, you're probably right. I just didn't stop to think about how it might look."

"Maybe you should go."

He froze, her words cutting like a scalpel. "You want me to leave Miami's Grace?"

"Oh, no! Not at all. But maybe you should take a week and go take flowers to your daughter."

He frowned, not expecting that suggestion. "Maybe someday."

"If you have other children, you might want them to—"

"I won't. I'm not having any more children."

Her head tilted. "Not ever?"

"No. Losing her was too hard." If he couldn't even visit his daughter's grave, how the hell would he be able to look into another baby's eyes without thinking of her—without wondering if that child, too, would be taken from him. Even the thought made a spurt of bile shoot up his throat.

She nodded. "I can't even imagine. But thank you for explaining."

"You're welcome." He heaved out a gust of air, relief washing over him. "So we're good?"

"I thought I did something wrong."

That was the problem. She hadn't. She'd done everything right. A little too right.

"Nope. Not at all." He smiled. "I didn't drive you to working too hard, did I?"

"Possibly."

"What?" Tension began building at the back of his head all over again.

"I was joking, Garret. But it wouldn't be a tragedy even if I did. Working actually helps clear my head—it takes my mind off myself."

"Using it to dull your pain can backfire, though. I know from experience."

"That won't happen to me."

"You know that for a fact?"

Her mouth twisted as she seemed to think about how to respond. "I won't drive when I'm exhausted. I'll take a cab. And at least I'm helping people in the process. I'm not burying myself in a bottle or drugs."

"You're right." He sat back and crossed an ankle over his knee. "And now I'll get off your case about it."

She laughed. "Thank you. So what are you going to do with your weekend? Take your new surfboard out for a spin?"

"I thought about it, but I don't think I'm proficient enough to go out on my own. Buying it was probably a mistake."

"It wasn't a mistake. Learning a new skill

is always good." There was an obvious hesitation before she added, "And it might even help your hand more than those therapy balls."

Her glance went to his desk, making him wish he'd put the balls away. He'd begun using them again, even though he wasn't sure why. "Surfing will? How?"

"It's a natural way to add to what you've already done." Ticking down on her fingers, she named a few ways. "Carrying your board helps with grasping skills. Paddling out to a wave—the water creates drag on your hand and fingers, like resistance bands would, but there's a better range of motion used in the ocean. Planting your hands on the surfboard when you pop up into your stance. You've said you have problems flexing the fingers on that hand. I noticed when we went out that you curled the fingers and used your fist. Why not flatten your hand as much as you can instead and let the weight of your body do the work? I would say do the same with push-ups, if you do them. It might hurt, but as long as your tendons aren't in danger of snapping, it can be a good way to coax them to lengthen."

She took a breath to continue, but he cut her off. "You'd make a great physical therapist. I hadn't thought about surfing being good for anything but recreation, but maybe you're right. You thought about all of this when we were out on the water?"

"I didn't until you said you'd bought a board. Swimming is always good exercise, and surfing works a lot of muscles in a lot of different ways. Why not use it to your benefit?"

"Why not indeed? I'll give it some thought."

"If you don't want to go by yourself, maybe we can set up one day a week when we spend a few hours out. I'll have to plan my schedule around the tides on weekends, if those are the only days off you get."

He wasn't sure spending more time with her outside work was a good idea, but since they'd gotten any baggage off the table in regard to the night they'd spent together, what could it hurt? They were both aware of the lingering attraction between them, so they'd be on guard now. Right?

"Weekends are my official days off, but I can sneak away for a few hours every now and then."

And that sounded a little suspect. But she knew what he meant.

He certainly wasn't opposed to the idea, even if he wasn't convinced his hand would reap much benefit from it. He could still go and have a good time.

"There are whole surfing communities, so it wouldn't have to be forever. Just until you meet some people. I do understand about not wanting to go out alone. I have the same problem, which is why I don't go out as much as I'd like to. So this will get me back into the groove as well."

He didn't see himself hanging out with the surfer crowd, but he didn't contradict her.

"I don't think you've ever lost your groove, from the way you looked out there."

She smiled. "Well, thanks. I think. But you don't have to be an expert surfer. There are people of all ages and abilities out there."

"Easy to say when you're one of the experts."

"I'm not. I just enjoy the sun and surf." She stood. "Let me check the surf reports and I'll come up with some options for some days next week. How does that sound?"

"Are you sure?"

He didn't want her to feel forced into babysitting him.

"I am. But only if you'll admit that it might actually help your hand."

He got to his feet as well. "I'm willing to admit the 'might' part, while retaining a dose of healthy skepticism."

The skepticism outweighed anything else at the moment. But doing something other than working and sitting at home would be good for him in general.

"That's all I'm asking."

"Sounds good, then."

He saw her to the door and closed it behind her before he could watch her head down the hallway, slim hips swinging as she went.

She was the one who'd offered, he reminded himself as doubts began popping up like surfers on their boards.

It was then that he remembered that images of popping up were the last ones he should be bringing to mind. Because the previous mental pictures of Addy on a surfboard were branded in his skull from here to eternity.

Okay, so Garret hadn't quite expected to be on the water the day after she mentioned juggling her schedule. But he was. And each time he paddled his board out, he was aware of the tension of the water on his bad hand, the way the gentle pressure coaxed his fingers to stretch and release in rhythmic strokes. In fact, where he had always used his right hand to compensate for the weakness in his left, he purposely began to pull harder with his bad hand, making his fingers come together to form a cup that moved more water. Tendons strained, muscles burned, but it wasn't painful.

He selected a wave in the distance and waited for it to arrive, then flopped his midsection onto his board and paddled. As soon as he felt that magical push, he flattened his hands on the board and tried to spring to his feet. Big mistake. Daggers stabbed at his fingers the second his weight fell on them and lights flashed behind his lids. He crashed into the water and came up sputtering, holding his hand to his chest as he trod water and waited for the agony to subside. Too much too fast.

Hell, this was a terrible idea.

Addy paddled over to where he was. "Are you okay?"

"Yes. It just hurt more than I expected

it to." He let his hand sink below the surface both to cool the burning and to hide the vague sense of embarrassment. He'd told her he didn't want to come out here alone, but he hadn't really thought through the ramifications of her seeing him in pain. He didn't like the feeling.

"Maybe try cupping your hand. I know I told you to try to keep it flat, but maybe somewhere in the middle of those two extremes would be better."

She was so matter-of-fact about it that it eased some of his misgivings.

The next time, he kept his fingers curled more so that his weight was distributed along the base of his palm rather than the fingers themselves. Then he was up, hands held as he'd seen others do to get his balance.

Addy had caught the wave behind his and dropped off further in to shore than he did, making her way back to where he was. "How was that? Better?"

"It's going to take some work, finding that balance between not protecting it and not hurting it."

"Isn't that the way with almost everything in life?"

He mulled over the words a time or two, then forced a lightness into his voice that he didn't quite feel. "Adding philosopher to your list of medical titles?" What she'd said had hit way too close to home. He was still struggling to find that balance in life. The balance of retreating behind a wall of steel to avoid emotional pain, and exposing too much of himself and getting stung for it.

Kind of like the night he'd spent at her house. He'd allowed himself to become vulnerable only to take off at a sprint at the mere mention of flowers on a grave. She'd implied that she'd been confused and hurt at the abrupt way he'd left.

He wasn't confused. But he was going to be more careful. The last thing he wanted was to accidentally cause Addy pain.

Sex might blur reality for a little while, but it soon showed back up, shining a spotlight on every character flaw he possessed.

And he was finding out his biggest flaw of all was running from his problems. He'd used work after Leticia died to flee from not only the pain of her death, but also the breakdown of his marriage. He swallowed. Maybe he was even using his position as administrator to run from the possibility of practicing medicine again.

"A philosopher? Not hardly. Just throwing out the first thought that came to mind. I seem to be good at that." She propped her chin on her board. "You up to catching a few more waves?"

Anything to keep from dissecting her words any more than he already had.

"I am. And thanks for coming with me today." He might not be sure of the wisdom of spending more time with her, but she was right about surfing being good for his hand. The muscles were aching slightly from the work. He normally used that hand as little as possible. Not only was it faster just to use his dominant hand for most things, it was also a way to keep the damaged hand out of sight. Running from the reality of his situation by hiding it away?

Just as he'd run from her house.

"You're welcome. I'm trying to turn over a new leaf of working less and enjoying life more, but it's going to take some time."

He couldn't argue with that. He'd been forced to go cold turkey when he'd had his accident, since he'd been unable to work at all, much less put in too many hours. But he'd made it through the worst of it. The desire to put in long hours was still there, but it no longer consumed him. Maybe his grief was fading. Or maybe he just never wanted to go through months of grueling physical therapy again.

While the waves were still decent, Garret worked on his hand during the pop up. Eventually, his digits said "enough" in no uncertain terms, and he was forced to call a halt to the day.

"I think I'm done." He carried his board out of the water and walked toward where Addy was already sitting on her towel, her hair in chaotic curls from the salt water.

Unlike their other trip to the beach, Addy's swimsuit was blue. And it was all one piece, this time. She'd even put a white lace cover-up over it as she sat on the sand.

Because of him?

He hoped not.

"You outlasted me, this time," she said, putting her hand over her eyes to look up at him. "How did it feel?"

"Like I've swallowed a couple more gallons of salt water, but I was able to actually stay upright longer than the last trip."

"So I saw. I thought you did great. And how's the hand?"

"Tired and sore. But it's a good kind of sore."

"Surf therapy. Kind of has a nice ring to it. You could start a whole new trend."

Laying his board down, he sat on the towel next to hers and leaned back slightly. The salt water drying on his skin caused a prickly tightening sensation that he combatted by rubbing his palm over his chest. "Thanks for this. I needed it."

"Any time."

He probably wasn't going to take her up on that. Because being with her here today—indulging in small talk and having her take a genuine interest in his hand—was taking its toll on his resolve.

He wanted her. Again. There was no doubt about that.

But to travel back down that road right now would be a mistake. His marriage had been a disaster. Addy's current marriage was a disaster. Neither one of them had the best track record in that area.

The truth was, Garret didn't know how to have a healthy relationship. He'd been so consumed with grief over his daughter's death that he'd added the final boulder, which had collapsed an already teetering marriage. Where shared pain might have drawn them together, his unbending selfishness had hurt both him and Patrice.

He wasn't sure enough of himself to know that he wouldn't do it again, given the right circumstances. He'd like to think he was done running, but until he was sure, he wasn't going to take that chance.

But what he *could* do was sit next to this particular woman and enjoy being with her. No strings. No commitments… No running.

"Garret, are you okay?"

"Sorry, my mind was on something else. Did you say something?"

"Just that Leo signed the divorce papers, so hopefully there will be no more scenes at the hospital."

Meaning she would stick around. Maybe she wasn't so unlike him after all. Hadn't she thought about leaving the hospital if things got too tough? Although that wasn't exactly the same thing as running. Was it?

"That has to be a relief."

"It's not exactly what I'd hoped for when I married him." She sat up and crossed her legs. "But it is what it is. There's no way to change it, and I wouldn't even if I could. I never really knew him. We never gave ourselves a chance to learn about each other before rushing into marriage."

He and Patrice hadn't rushed in, but the marriage had ended just the same. "Relationships are hard under the best of circumstances."

"You sound like you speak from experience."

"Let's just say my marriage didn't survive my stupidity. Not that it was all that strong to begin with. But Leticia's death was the final straw. I started working, had the accident… and the rest is history, as they say."

She frowned. "You were grieving." She pulled her cover up closer around her, and he noticed the shadows were growing longer. How long had he been out there anyway?

He glanced down at his watch. "Hell, I'm sorry, Addy. I had no idea it was almost seven o'clock."

Only a few intrepid surfers were still out

there trying to find a wave to make it worth their while.

"It's fine. I had a good time."

"Yeah. So did I." He really had and that bothered him on a level he was afraid to examine. Because it was no secret to either of them that he wanted her physically. But now he was enjoying her company more than ever. And the thing he was afraid of most was that he might even come to want her friendship. Might already be on his way to getting it.

And at this moment, Garret had no idea what to do about it. Or how to stop it from becoming a reality he could no longer ignore.

CHAPTER NINE

HER PERIOD WAS OVERDUE. By almost four days.

Standing at the auction in her new dress, she found herself shivering.

It was so unlike her body that she'd taken a pregnancy test this morning even though she knew it was too early to know.

He'd used a condom.

But, looking back, neither one of them had wanted to break that intimate connection between them. Had it been long enough to cause a leak?

The rehearsal yesterday had gone smoothly, but her life right now was pretty much a blur of which she could remember nothing.

God, what if she was pregnant?

Hadn't she just been thinking about the fact that she and Leo had never had children and that she was getting older? Could she have somehow willed her body to find a way?

And then along came Garret, revving her hormones up to a fever pitch. Had the fates conspired against her?

She swallowed. So far she hadn't seen him tonight, but she was pretty sure he had to be here somewhere in the crush of tuxedos and dark suits.

There was no way she was going to tell him unless her test revealed a pink plus sign. She actually clasped her hands and sent up a quick prayer that that would not happen.

There were a lot more people than she'd expected there to be, so many that it was standing room only in the conference center of the swanky hotel. After the auction there was a buffet of finger foods and a dessert line. She wanted nothing to do with either of those two things.

"Addy, you all set?"

The low voice behind her was both familiar and strange. She spun around to find Garret standing there in a dazzling white shirt and the requisite tux. Only he did for it what few men here could do: transform it into a sexy, meet-me-at-the-dessert-bar siren call.

One she was going to resist with all her might. But at least it made her feel better about things. She wasn't pregnant. She couldn't be.

He glanced at her dress and his Adam's apple bobbed dangerously.

"Wow. Green suits you. You should wear it more often."

That made her smile, despite the craziness that had gone on in her head. "Well, since I'm an ER doc, white lab coats are kind of the color of the day. But I'll keep it in mind. You look great too."

"I'm serious. We better make sure no one thinks you're up for bid."

"I'll be sure to set them straight." Something inside her shifted, his words giving her a shot of confidence she'd been lacking since Leo's unfaithfulness. She might have backed out, if she hadn't promised him she would be here. And since she'd promised him she wouldn't put in crazy hours at work, here she was. She needed to be somewhere that she didn't have time to think.

At least she hadn't been worried about a

possible pregnancy at the beach last week. She was glad. It had been a wonderful day. And talk about confident... Each time he'd paddled out, he was becoming more and more proficient at the mechanics. Watching him from shore had been a treat.

It wasn't beautiful, yet, but that would come with time—the flowing motion of becoming almost one with your board.

She was proud of him. And a little nervous that she cared enough to feel that way.

"How's your hand?" she asked.

He lifted it and made a slow painful fist with it. "It'll never be normal and I might be absolutely crazy, but I think I see a little improvement in flexibility."

"That's great! Now you just need to keep up the good work."

"Do you want something to drink before we get started? We still have a few minutes to go."

"I'd love one, actually. Just something refreshing." She hesitated before adding, "Non-alcoholic."

You are not pregnant, Addy.

"I know just the thing. I'll be right back."

Thank God he hadn't seemed to notice that

pause before she'd specified that she didn't want any alcohol.

Addy watched him head toward the cash bar. His back was ramrod straight, eyes on where he was headed. He was a proud man.

Realizing your surgical career was over couldn't have been an easy thing to get to grips with. But he seemed to have made the shift. He was doing a great job at the hospital, but there was a part of her that wondered if he wasn't selling himself short. Taking the easy road, rather than the best one.

Leo had done that. He'd kind of skated along in his job, content just to do the bare minimum required.

Not fair, Addy. Garret is nothing like Leo.

And it wasn't up to her to tell her boss what he should or shouldn't be doing. He had to decide that for himself.

When he came back, he was carrying a margarita-sized glass containing something with orange on top and pink on the bottom. It sported a little umbrella. His own drink of choice was sparkling water.

"I bet that got some looks. What is it?" She took the drink from him, intrigued by what he thought she might like.

"Pomegranate and citrus."

"Sounds delicious." She touched the glass to her lips, expecting the strong taste of orange juice to assail her taste buds. But this was sharper, notes of lemon and maybe grapefruit cutting through the sweet. She took another sip. And yes, there was the pomegranate. "I love it. Thank you."

"I was hoping you would." He took her arm. "Come see the auction items."

Tropical-themed cabanas were set up in a ring, each containing a different genre of items. Whoever had chosen what went where had an eye for design. It was amazing. There were things that ranged from a children's book basket topped with a cheerful teddy bear to spa treatments. In the jewelry cabana, she spotted her pearls laid out among piles of faux oysters. The attention to detail took her breath away.

"Is it always this beautiful?"

"Yes. Last year the theme was an ocean voyage. They set everything up like a cruise ship, complete with a buffet line and fake pools."

"Local businesses pay for all the decorations?" She remembered the auction brochure listing sponsors and what each had helped with.

"Yes. They get some advertising in, as well as knowing they're helping the hospital expand its services to the community."

He steered her over toward another part of the room, where a large screen flashed images from the hospital, mostly the children's ward since this auction would help fund equipment and needed upgrades.

"Look!" She gestured toward the slide-show. Although she'd put in a request for Grace's family to be included, she could hardly believe the pictures they'd come up with. Grace, her mom, and the children from the house fire were displayed. One picture showed the family in the lobby as they were getting ready to leave. She and Garret were there. Their eyes were focused on each other, and she had a slight smile curving her lips. Heat rose in her chest and suffused her face, but the image winked out as quickly as it appeared. The last picture was the family in what looked like the kitchen of their home. They were smiling, and—a sudden pricking behind her eyes came out of nowhere. Grace was holding baby Matthew, something she'd refused to do when they were at the hospital. Before she could say anything to Garret the picture was gone.

"Did you see that?" Her voice came out as a whisper.

"I did." His hand touched the small of her back and stayed there. "I went to see them and asked if I could take the picture."

"You went to their house? Why didn't you say anything? I would have liked to have known how they were doing."

"I wanted to surprise you."

A lump formed in her throat and stayed there, refusing to go down even when she took a sip of her drink. She did her best not to imagine herself holding a baby like Matthew in the near future.

She wanted that. So very badly. But not like this. She wanted it with someone who loved her. Someone that she loved in return.

"You did surprise me. In the best possible way." She watched other families come on the screen. Patients she didn't know. "They were okay with these pictures being displayed? I don't even remember anyone taking the pictures at the hospital."

"The photographers were working pro

bono. They come when they have holes in their schedules and shoot candids for us. We get permission obviously for any that would end up here at the auction."

"How were they—Grace and her family—when you saw them?"

"They were good. Even Grace. She seems to have worked through whatever she was dealing with when she was here."

She glanced at the screen, hoping the loop would work its way back around so she could see them again. "Their kitchen?"

He shrugged. "It was repaired."

Why had he said it like that? As if it didn't matter at all. It certainly did for that family. "Did they have insurance?"

"No. I don't believe so." The response was quick. He somehow knew they didn't have insurance. But how, unless he'd asked? Unless he'd—

Her heart clenched.

"You paid for the repairs, didn't you? It's why you went over to the house."

"It doesn't matter."

Those familiar faces came scrolling by again. She watched as from one frame to the next, they transformed from tragic to healed.

She swallowed and turned to look at him. "It does matter. It matters very, very much, and I—"

A booming voice interrupted her. "Welcome to the tenth annual Miami's Grace Hospital fund-raising auction. If those who are a part of our volunteer force would take their places, we can get started."

"That's us," he said.

Garret hadn't wanted his deed made public. Why?

Whatever the reason, it made her respect him all the more. Along with that thought came a quick flash of something else that she soon banished.

Right now, there was no time to think about anything other than her job. She had to find her cabana—of beach items, of all things. That had to have been Garret's doing as well. To go along with her surfing. Well, she certainly would feel more at home there than in the fashion cabana.

He'd said he liked her choice of dress, though. She glanced down. The scooped neckline was a little lower than she was normally comfortable with, showing a hint of cleavage at the top. But it didn't go below the tan line from her bathing suit, so that had to be something, right?

The bodice clung all the way down to her upper thighs, where it suddenly swooshed out into a full skirt that swirled with every move she made. It also clung to her derrière in a way that was a little disconcerting, but the salesperson swore it was all the rage right now, that it was supposed to fit snugly.

She'd decided to step outside her comfort zone and buy it. Wow, she remembered when she and Garret had had that conversation about comfort zones and he'd joked about not being as sturdy as he used to be. Looking at him now, she couldn't see anything in him that was anything but sturdy. He was strong and compassionate—even if he didn't really want anyone to know it.

Why hadn't she met him five years ago, instead of Leo?

Well, maybe because he'd been married and had suffered one of the biggest tragedies a person could go through: losing a child.

He'd been a different person back then.

So had she.

The auctioneer introduced Garret and had him go up to the podium to say a few words of welcome as people made their way to their seats, auction paddles in hand. The short speech he gave was flawless and confident and edged with a sincerity that couldn't be faked. He believed in what he was doing. Maybe he wasn't just "settling" as she'd basically accused him of doing.

His injured hand was on the podium, the slanted surface putting it out of sight of anyone except those who knew him well. Would these people be surprised to know that he had donned board shorts and carried a surfboard into the water?

Probably. Because right now he looked like the consummate executive. Confident, unruffled and perfectly groomed, his dark hair swept back from his forehead, not a strand out of place.

But they didn't know him as she did.

And Addy liked that. Liked seeing a side of him that no one else would or could.

She found herself staring, and was pretty sure an army of women in the audience also had a speculative eye on him. He was sexy. And unattached.

That made her come back to earth with a bump. Yes, she might know things about him that other people didn't, but it didn't make a difference. She had no claim on him, nor did she want one.

Even if a certain little someone might be lurking unseen who did have a claim on him.

She banished the thought as quickly as it appeared.

So, if one of these wealthy patrons wanted to take him home for the evening, she wouldn't care?

She would. She'd want to scratch the woman's eyes out. And that drove her crazy with irritation.

Whatever this little crush thing she had going on, it needed to be over and done with pronto. Because, if against all odds she did wind up pregnant, she was setting herself up for a very big fall. One that would hurt more than anything Leo had ever done to her.

I'm not having any more children.

Wasn't that what he'd said?

Garret ended his speech and a round of applause followed as he signaled the auction was set to begin. Addy found herself shaky and nervous, for more reasons than just holding up auction items.

But there was a lot riding on this event, so

she needed to put aside her problems and pull herself together. A lot of kids like Matthew would get a chance to have an accurate diagnosis thanks to new modern equipment. They deserved it. And Matthew's family couldn't afford to pay for those kinds of things; they could barely afford to put food on the table. But this crowd could.

She willed the bidding to be fierce and competitive as the auctioneer worked his way through the first cabana: tools and DIY items. The big-ticket item in that lot was a flatbed trailer perfect for hauling everything from lawn equipment to camping supplies. It went for over a thousand dollars.

Addy hadn't had a chance to look through the bid book, which listed each item and gave a suggested retail price. Maybe she should have.

Bidding was closed on the first cabana and moved to the second, which was housewares. Bidding went quickly on that one and then they were on Addy's turf. She got into place and waited for the auctioneer to name the first item—a set of gardening tools—lifting each item as it was named until the gavel came down with the words "*Sold* to—"

and the bidder's number was entered into the record.

There were thirty articles ranging from snorkeling equipment to a long board, which was beautifully handcrafted and had an estimated bidding price of twelve hundred dollars. She wouldn't have minded owning that board herself, but it was probably against the rules to bid on something in her own group. Using the carry straps that were included with the board, she put the webbed bands over her shoulder and demonstrated how to transport it, unable to resist running her fingers across the highly polished surface. She probably looked ridiculous carrying it around in her dress, but it didn't matter. She caught Garret's eye from where he stood to the side of the cabanas. He gave her a smile and a nod that turned something in her tummy all liquid.

She blinked back to what she was doing as the bidding continued to climb. She couldn't very well demonstrate how to stand on it because she could damage the fins on the hard floor, so she had to suffice with just moving around with it. The winning bid was almost seventeen hundred dollars. The board was worth every penny of that. With a sigh, she propped it back against the fake palm tree, allowing her fingers to trail across the warm surface one final time before moving on to the last item.

When her section was finished, she was able to slide once again into the background. Garret met her at the edge of the crowd. "Good job out there. That was a beautiful board."

"Thanks. It looks like it's going well. And, yes, that board was the most beautiful thing I've ever seen."

"I can think of something even more gorgeous."

When she jerked to look at him, his gaze was fixed on the auctioneer.

Ha! Had she actually thought he was talking about her?

Dream on, Addy. There are all kinds of beautiful people and items in this room.

"Any idea how much the auction has brought in so far?"

"There's no official tally right now, and people can give a monetary donation without actually bidding on anything. But since it's more exciting to dress up and come to the auction than to just mail in a check, there'll be a time for that. The auctioneer will call out different amounts and the attendees will raise their paddles, committing to give that amount. It's almost as exciting as the bidding itself. And the whole event is a good way to get the hospital's name out there."

"I can't believe I've never come to one of these before. I like it. And it's good to see the generosity of people in the community. It looks like they really love Miami's Grace."

"South Beach has always supported the hospital. We couldn't do what we do without them."

Garret went with her to wait in line for a plate of finger food, ignoring her protest that the guests should go first. "Most of them already have their plates, if you look around the room. When they're not bidding, they're eating, so it's fine."

They got their tidbits and Addy got another pomegranate citrus drink, and then they found a place to sit in the vendors' area, where most of the auction items had come from. So far none of the donated items had gone without some kind of bid, so the product vendors would go back to their places of business empty-handed, a very good thing for both the hospital and the companies who made the donations.

"You said you don't have a tally right now, but how much does the hospital normally get from the auctions? I haven't paid attention, although I know I should have."

"A hundred thousand wouldn't be out of the ordinary."

"Out of the ordinary. I'd say that was extraordinary. Does the hospital already have plans for the money?"

He dropped his damaged hand below the table and picked up a finger sandwich, giving it a dubious look before taking a bite.

Addy laughed. "It's cucumber. I've heard they're pretty much standard fare at these swanky affairs."

"I thought you hadn't been to one of these before."

"Not to the hospital's, but I do put on a dress every once in a while. Just not very often."

His lips twisted to the side. "I'm not sure that longboard would have brought in as much as it did without you serving as its backdrop."

"I don't know about that—it was worth all of that and probably more." She decided to change the subject before she started thinking funny thoughts again. "So the money brought in will go for…"

"We have a wish list by price. It's in the auction pamphlet. It helps people know where their bidding dollars are going. It works very well."

"I can see how it would." She hadn't looked beyond the cover of the pamphlet, since it had been hard to get past the picture of her pearls. "Do you like giving speeches?"

"Not particularly, but I do what needs to be done."

"Yes, and you do it very well. So well that I think I owe you an apology."

This time he turned to face her, sitting back in his seat. "For what?"

"For trying to convince you that you should teach, that you could still do something useful in the medical world. I was wrong. Not that you couldn't teach or do any number of things. But I'm coming to realize that this *is* useful. I just never realized how much so."

"Forgiven. And maybe you were right on some level. Maybe taking this job was a cop-out. But there really are a lot of things that need to be done to keep the hospital running smoothly. And I'll never perform surgery again, no matter how much use I regain of my hand."

"No, but you're so gifted—" She stopped herself. "And there I go again. Sorry."

Two more cabanas had closed out bidding.

The jewelry cabana was next and she suddenly stood. "Do you mind if I go outside for some air?"

She didn't really want to see the pearls or hear the bidding on them. She wasn't attached to them, and, right now, all they brought back were bad memories. Memories much better forgotten.

"Of course. Everything okay?"

"Yes. I just don't want to be here for this part. I know it's stupid. It's just—"

"Not stupid at all. If you want some company, I won't be missed for a minute or two."

She didn't answer—because she wasn't sure how she felt about being around him right now—so she just let him decide for himself. He ended up following her out and they soon found themselves across the street on the sidewalk, leaning against the rail, the scent of the ocean carried in on a gentle breeze.

"I love that smell. Have never gotten tired of it."

"The fragrance of seaweed?"

"Funny. No. The salt. The smell of damp earth and clean air that comes with living near the water."

He smiled, turning around and bracing his elbows on the low wall. "I will admit that, as crowded as it is in South Beach, there are times like this, when you get the impression that life isn't moving as fast as it is in places like New York. There's time to sit back and enjoy the beauty, even on a night as busy as this one."

"And days when you can just take your surfboard out and make any day into one of those quiet reflective times."

"Yes, there is that."

"Do you miss New York? I've never been there, so I have no idea what it's like outside of television shows." Was she curious about whether he might go back there someday? Especially with what he'd said about not putting flowers on his daughter's grave.

"Some parts, but not much. I miss seeing

the seasons change. I miss sometimes feeling like you have a bubble around you—that despite the thousands of people passing by, you live in this isolated little spot where no one enters unless you invite them in. South Beach is friendly. And sometimes there aren't boundaries."

She gulped. Sometimes there weren't boundaries in more ways than one. She forced herself to keep talking, as if there weren't this little pain inside that just kept getting bigger and bigger.

"I never thought of it that way, but, yes, you're right. People socialize here in a casual, carefree way."

"I was surprised to find out that South Beach isn't always just about the beach. Or the ocean, although that's a big draw. I actually do like it here."

"Enough to stay here for the rest of your life?" Oh, Lord, why had she just asked that?

"I think so. The jury is still out on that."

That little pain widened, radiating from her heart out to the surrounding areas.

"I can't imagine the hospital without you."

"I can't imagine it without you either." His words were so soft that she had to tilt her head to capture them all. His arm looped around her waist for several seconds, and that ache inside went from uncomfortable to giddy. "Addy, I shouldn't even ask this, but will you meet me after this is all over with?"

Was he asking her to—?

This was the moment of truth. She was pretty sure she knew what was behind that request. She'd be pretty devastated, actually, if she was wrong. And despite everything, there was an answering need inside herself.

"Yes," she breathed.

It was as if all that fear and those countless admonitions this evening had never happened. She wanted to be with this man, wanted the auction to be done and on her way. But of course it wasn't.

She leaned her head against his jacket, reveling in the weight of his arm around her waist, the heady masculine scent that drifted up on ocean currents, the way his breath ruffled across her hair.

This was why it was so hard to resist him. Why she didn't want to resist him.

The moment grew longer and longer, until she felt his lips brush the top of her head. "We'd better go back in before we're missed."

She was pretty sure she wouldn't be missed at all, but she knew he still had some things he needed to do before they could go.

Once inside, she forced her eyes to stay focused up front, even as she sensed Garret's impatience beside her.

She understood it completely—felt the exact same way.

"They're motioning for me up front. I'll be back in a minute." He curved his index finger around hers and squeezed. "Do not go anywhere."

"I won't." There was no way she was leaving now. She wanted to be here when he came back, wanted to go wherever he wanted to take her.

He gave his closing remarks, thanking everyone for coming and promising they would post the totals for the auction on the hospital's website.

"Enjoy your night. There is still plenty of food left and the bar will remain open for a while longer. When you're ready, you can turn in your bid cards and collect your items. For those things which are too large to carry or won't fit in your vehicle, we have asked a shipping company to set up a booth in the lobby. They can help you arrange transportation. Thank you again for coming. Miami's Grace Hospital is grateful to each of you."

He left the dais to applause, striding through the crowd, stopping to shake hands here and there and smile as people talked to him. He never gave the impression he was in a hurry, gave his undivided attention to each person that crossed his path, but with each step he managed to take, he was keenly aware of where she was. His trajectory told her that, because he never wavered or veered off course.

All she could do was stand there, a sick sense of anticipation building in her belly. Because once he arrived and they were on their way, things were going to be off the charts.

And she was terrified of what that might mean.

CHAPTER TEN

ALTHOUGH GARRET'S APARTMENT was in a nice area of town, it was sparsely furnished. None of that mattered right now. All she cared about were the long, slow kisses that he was planting on her mouth.

They'd made it through the door, and then he'd backed her up against a nearby wall, tossing his keys onto a side table.

Then he'd kissed her.

Was still kissing her, hands pressed on the wall on either side of her head. He was leaning in. Taking his time, unlike at her place when everything had seemed so frantic and desperate.

Garret had voted for his place.

And she had readily agreed. She needed to be somewhere where she could remove herself from reality—needed to find out what, if anything, she meant to him. In case the unthinkable was actually true.

He eased her a couple of inches away from the wall and his hands went to the back of her dress. He found the zipper and she could feel the wrist of his damaged hand pressing the fabric at her nape as the other hand slid the tab slowly down, all the way past her butt.

When he let go, the fabric fell away, pooling on the floor around her feet.

She didn't care. Didn't want to pick it up, too entranced by the continued short touches of mouth to mouth. She squirmed, trying to deepen the pressure, but it didn't work. "Shh, I want to enjoy it this time."

She smiled against his lips. "Are you saying you didn't last time?" He followed her words with kisses, teasing her mercilessly.

"I enjoyed it very much. But I wanted more. I still do." His teeth nipped at her jawline. "Now step out of your shoes. One at a time."

He backed up a pace and watched as she used one shoe to loosen the other along the back. Then she let it drop on the floor. The other shoe came off just as easily.

She was barefoot before him, and, boy, did

he seem to tower over her. "Do you need help with your tie?"

"I need help. But not with that." A quick flash of his teeth as he reached up with one hand and loosened the knot, slipping a finger under the tab until it hung free.

How had he tied it in the first place? She'd thought maybe he'd used a clip-on, but she should have known he wouldn't take the easy way out.

"Now the buttons." She moistened her lips and waited to see if he would do her bidding.

He did, undoing three.

She shook her head. "More." Then she noticed his sleeves. Buttoned with jeweled cuff links. She reached forward to touch one of them. "How?"

"I had the sleeves custom made just wide enough that I can slide my hand through it. My dry cleaner takes the cuff links out and puts them back once the shirt is laundered."

"You must really trust your cleaner."

"I do." As he'd talked, he'd been slowly undoing the buttons of his shirt all the way down to the cummerbund. "Now your turn."

"Uh…you have more clothes than I do. It's still your turn."

He reached behind him and ripped the Velcro that held the black satin band, letting it drop to the floor. "Now you."

Well, since she was standing there in just a lacy one-piece bodyshaper—one that had boasted no panty lines—that was going to be hard. "Still you."

His rough laugh made her tummy ripple with need. "You can't blame a guy for trying." He pulled his shirt out of his dress trousers and finished undoing the buttons, letting it hang open. Then, when she shook her head, he slid it off his shoulders and let it drop to the floor.

His chest was now bare, just the slightest dusting of hair in the middle—a dark shadow that trailed down his flat torso and disappeared behind his waistband. All things she hadn't been able to notice the last time because of the rush.

"Yes. I like that."

"Are we even now?"

In answer, she slid the straps of her undergarment down her arms, letting them hang loose as she peeled a little bit of the bodice down. Just enough to entice him. She hoped.

She'd never been the best at doing a sexy striptease designed to drive men wild.

At least, she had never gotten the hang of it with Leo, who wanted an elaborate show, but did very little in return. But Garret made her want to be sexy. Made her want to do a little give and take.

"You're killing me, honey."

"Shoes and socks?"

It was working. He did seem to like it.

He toed out of his shoes and reached down to undo his socks, tucking them into his black patent leathers.

"Okay, now—"

"Pants." She grinned a challenge at him.

"Don't make me come over there, Addy."

"Or what?"

God, her body was responding to all of this verbal foreplay, nipples pressing hard against the fabric of her shaper, a familiar tingling starting up in other places. She was ready for him to grab her up and get this show on the road.

He took a step closer, and her fingers reached for the straps on the last thing she was wearing. Okay, if he wanted to play hardball, she could definitely match him play for play. She tugged at it, suddenly wishing she'd worn tiny underwear instead, because she remembered just how snug this thing had been when she'd put it on. But she did it, stepping out of it with a triumphal glance at him, only to freeze in place.

His face had gone completely still and he swallowed hard. "You are so…lovely."

Lovely. That was good, right? Then why the hesitation before the word had come out?

"T-trousers?"

Where had that stutter come from?

Garret frowned. "What's wrong?"

"Just having a moment of insecurity, that's all." Her throat worked as she struggled to swallow back a rush of tears. She was too afraid to tell him the whole truth, because she herself didn't yet know.

Then he was there, grabbing her up in an embrace that was as tight as his earlier kisses had been tender. There was no mistaking his erection pressed hard into her thigh. "Don't. No insecurity. Feel what you do to me."

He cupped her face and tilted her head to look at him. "There are so many adjectives I could have chosen. Beautiful. Gorgeous. Sexy. *Hot.* There's one for the books.

And they all would have been true. Every single one."

Her body went slack with relief. She had no idea why she'd suddenly felt as if she wasn't good enough. Maybe wondering how she compared to the mother of his child. Wondered how he would react if she too became the mother of his child. But his quick move to allay her fears had done just that, more than making up for her silly fears. He made her feel beautiful and all the other adjectives he'd mentioned.

"Just love me, Garret. That's all I need right now."

"Gladly."

With that, he swept her up in his arms and headed back to a different area of the apartment, past a living room and a leather couch. Down a hallway with two closed doors. He opened the first one and revealed a huge bed with four pine columns that ended just above the mattress. A bed that had no history with her, none at all. It was a blank slate. And she couldn't wait to put some writing on that slate.

He laid her down. Pulled his wallet from his back pocket and finished stripping the rest of the way. This time she didn't have to help. Maybe her zipper had smoothed the way for him. He seemed more secure himself this time. Whatever it was, she loved it.

Loved *hi*—

Her eyes slammed shut on the word before it fully formed.

No. Not right now. She could dissect feelings and possibilities later, but, for this moment in time, she just wanted to be with him.

She looked at him again. The thumb of his right hand was in the waistband of his briefs, his eyes on hers.

"Do it."

Then he was out of them, kicking them away and picking up his wallet again. For one infinitesimal second she wished he didn't have to use it. Wished they could just love each other without anything coming between them.

But they had to. If she wasn't pregnant already, she didn't want to become pregnant. Maybe, despite what he'd said in his office, he'd be able to go that route with someone else. Someday.

Why not with her?

Later, remember?

Unaware of her thoughts, he found a condom and laid it on a pillow near the headboard. She decided to make light of what, for her, was becoming a moment that was fraught with dangers she didn't want to face. "Just one?"

He smiled, coming onto the bed and pressing his body against hers, breasts flattening against his hard chest. She gloried in the feeling, reveled in not spoiling this moment with her hopes and fears.

"Don't worry—I have more where that came from." He rested his pelvis against hers. "And more where *that* came from."

Then his mouth was back on hers and he was kissing her as if he couldn't get enough, right hand exploring her, running over her breasts, down her rib cage, cupping her hip.

"Use the other one."

He came up. Looked down at her face. "Excuse me?"

Terrified he was going to be angry with her, but needing this so very much, she licked her lips. "Use your other hand. I want to feel it on me."

His eyes hardened slightly, and he acted as if he was going to get up. To run. "I can't."

Before he could go anywhere, she caught the wrist of his damaged hand and held on tight. "Use it, Garret. Please."

She lifted it to her chest, just above her breasts, and dragged the curled fingers against her skin. "Can they feel? Do they have sensation?"

"Yes." The word was rough-edged and seemed to be hauled up from some dark pit within him. This was a critical moment. He would either reject this…reject her, or he would open himself up and allow her to take everything. In the same way she was willing to give everything.

She touched her breast with it, using her own hands to guide him over the nipple. The sensation hit her hard and she arched, moaning.

"God, Addy. What are you doing to me?" Then he pulled his hand free from her grip.

Just when she thought she might have ruined everything, he took up where she left off, allowing his ruined digits to slide against her. He didn't cup anything or try to grasp, just let her skin provide tactile stimulation. The idea that she might be the first person to ask this of him was heady and it brought her to the very edge of the world.

If he could handle this, surely he'd be able to handle anything else she might throw at him.

His eyes slid closed as he continued to explore, and she hoped it felt as good to him as it did to her. She wanted this man. Wanted everything he had to give. When his fingers brushed over the curls at the apex of her thighs his eyelids jerked apart. "I don't think I can wait."

"Then don't. Don't." She reached around and grabbed the condom off the pillow and tore into it. Then she handed him the contents and held his damaged hand where it had stopped, keeping it there as he used his other hand to roll the latex sheath over his hard flesh.

She slowly spread her legs and slid his fingers a little lower. She bit her lip, breath coming in short bursts as she drew him closer and closer. "Feel it, Garret. Feel—" She exploded in a rush, pressing his hand hard against her as the contractions raged inside her.

Then he was right there, thrusting hard and fast, groaning against her throat as he went off a few seconds later; he kept pumping until he was spent, pace gradually slowing, while he pressed tiny kisses against her jaw, her cheek, her mouth. And then it was over, his body melting into hers, puffs of air sliding over her ear.

"Hell, Addy. Holy hell."

"Are you okay?" She tipped her head back so she could look in his face, worried about the tone of his voice.

"Okay? *Okay?*" He gave a laugh that lit her soul and turned her world upside down. "I don't think I'll ever be okay again."

He kissed her chin. "And I mean that in the best way possible. I have never felt like that in my life."

If he could just hold on to that thought.

She pulled in a huge lungful of air and released it as a wave of happiness spilled over her. "There are lots of ways to rehab that hand. I have a few more tricks up my sleeve."

"A few? I'm afraid to even imagine." He wrapped an arm around her back and rolled so he was on bottom and she was on top. "I don't want to squash you."

"You weren't. But I like the way you think."

And with that, she covered his mouth with hers and kissed him all over again.

Five tests were lined up on her bathroom counter.

Five reminders that the happiness of one night might not look the same two days later.

And it didn't. Not at all.

Addy huddled beneath the bubbles in her tub and trembled, her mind frantically working through all kinds of scenarios. Maybe he would be thrilled—would leap from his chair and kiss her senseless, tell her that he loved her as much as she loved him.

Because, yes, she did love him. Had realized it while they were making love. She'd tried to blot it out, to pretend it wasn't real, but the sensation hadn't faded away the next day. It had been there when she'd woken up to the smell of bacon and eggs—the very meal she'd tried to fix him all those weeks ago. In fact, she'd come out of the bedroom wearing one of his button-down shirts, saying she hoped he didn't mind. His answer had sent a shiver through her. A very different shiver than what she was now experiencing.

"Mind?" he'd said with a slow smile. "I

don't know. What would you do if I said yes, that I minded very much?"

A weird giddy sound had broken loose from her throat and wrapped around her. "Well, I guess I'd just have to take it off, then. Very slowly."

The wordplay had soon turned into another kind of play altogether. And she'd hoped… So hoped…

But he'd never said the words. And she'd tried to not care.

Until today.

She lifted a palmful of suds, and with a quick puff from her lungs sent them up into the air. What was once a single cohesive mass broke into distinct sections, which floated in different directions. Some popped and disappeared forever. Some joined with other bubbles. But the original unit was gone forever.

Kind of like Humpty Dumpty. Once broken, he could never be made whole again.

Was that what would happen to her and Garret? Not that they could even be considered a unit. Not yet. Maybe not ever.

Her eyes went back to the counter. Would her news shatter any possibility of a future with him?

But if he cared about her, would those tests matter that much? Maybe it would precipitate something good, rather than the disaster she was imagining.

She twisted her hair and clipped it higher so she could lie against the smooth surface at the back of the tub. Her hands dipped beneath the surface and skimmed over her stomach.

Pregnant.

But how?

It had to have been from that first time they were together. Maybe the condom was old. Maybe they'd just been careless at some point—or maybe it had simply failed. It happened. You heard stories about things like this all the time. Right?

Those plastic strips caught her eye again. Five tests said that she was now one of those statistics.

And she was happy. Scared, but, oh, so happy. God, she shouldn't be. She should be upset and angry and confused.

But she saw everything with a clarity that had been lacking before. She wanted this baby. Had wanted a child for a very long time, even when her ex-husband hadn't. The fact that it was Garret's and not Leo's? Even

better. At least it belonged to a man she re-
spected. A man who'd already had a child
and had loved that child deeply. He was made
to be a father, no matter what his response to
this particular pregnancy might be.

I'm not having any more children.

Not ever?

No.

That conversation burned across her memory banks, searing everything in its path. He
might not have planned—or even wanted—
to have any more kids, but fate was taking
that decision out of his hands.

Surely he would love the child, once he
found out about it.

Wouldn't he?

The shaking that had subsided a minute
ago started up all over again.

She had to tell him. It would be wrong to
withhold this kind of information. He had a
right to know. And a right to choose what to
do with the information.

She wrapped her arms around her midsection as if already protecting the tiny life that
was just taking root inside her.

One thing was certain. His reaction would
go one of two ways and it would determine

the course of their future interactions—or lack thereof.

Either he was going to welcome the news—even if he was initially dismayed or fearful. Or—and this was the possibility that had woken her in a cold sweat for the last two nights. Or Garret was going to run for the hills as fast as he possibly could.

CHAPTER ELEVEN

GARRET SCANNED THE READOUT, trying to decipher what he was looking at, but he was unable to concentrate on much of anything right now.

It had been two days since he'd kissed Addy goodbye in front of her house after taking her home. He had no more answers today than he'd had after seeing her standing there in his white dress shirt. There had been turmoil then. There was turmoil now.

It was as if he'd been shot through the heart, something changing inside him.

But what?

He wasn't sure. And wasn't sure he really wanted to know. He'd vowed to give himself one more day and then track her down long enough to talk. No easy feat.

She seemed to be avoiding him as much as he was evading her.

And the spikes for those two days…

As bad or worse than they'd been that day he called her into his office. The day she dropped those pearls, setting a big machine into motion.

He didn't know what had made him look at the staff hours' readout. But he had. Maybe to see if their night together had had as profound an effect on her as it had on him.

From what he could see, it had. Only he wasn't sure what it meant.

She was back to keeping killer hours. In the days since they'd spent the night together, she'd put in five hours of overtime. It was a lot.

He could understand staying to finish up a case, but this was more than that.

Something was seriously bothering her. Or worrying her.

Well, she wasn't the only one. He was worried too. Only he wasn't sure what to do about it.

Talk to her?

And say what? "Listen, Addy, about that night…"

That was where his ability to reason fell apart. His brain cells had evidently developed a serious leak when it came to figuring things out.

Sitting back in his chair, he put his hands on the desk and stared at his damaged one. His injury was what came of getting his priorities in the wrong place. He couldn't afford to do that again—to bury his pain in his work.

What did Addy have to bury?

He had no idea, but one of them needed to drum up the courage to break the ice and start figuring this thing out.

He stood to do just that, only to stop in his tracks when a knock sounded at his door.

Surely not.

But maybe...

"Come in." He frowned at how eager those words sounded. Hell, it might not even be Addy.

He needed to slow down and think through anything he might say, if it was her. Preferably *before* he gave voice to it.

His intuition proved correct when Addy's head peeked around the corner. "Do you have a minute?"

"I was just coming to find you, actually."

"You were?" She entered the room, her face paler than he ever remembered seeing it. Was she ill?

"Yes. Have a seat, please." He stood. "Are you okay?"

"I think so. I'm not really sure."

A rush of concern went through him. "What's going on?"

She didn't sit, as he'd asked. And something about the way she stood there made an alarm go off in his head. He decided to stay on his feet as well, just in case he needed to catch her. She looked ready to break apart at any second.

"I have something to tell you."

"Okay." He suddenly wasn't so sure he wanted to hear it, but those brain cells still weren't working at a hundred percent.

Instead of answering, Addy dropped some kind of white plastic object onto the center of his desk. It bounced a time or two then came to a stop in front of him.

He frowned at it for several seconds. Then a frisson of fear went up his spine as he recognized it. Evidently a few of those cells were still functioning. And now he wished they weren't.

"What is this?" The rough, hoarse quality of his voice gave away his thoughts. He didn't let his eyes focus on the test, kept them purposely averted to a spot just beside it, where the exercise balls lay.

Something about the disparity between those two things struck him as hilarious, in a way that was anything but funny.

There was only one reason for her to have brought that in his office.

He swallowed. No. There was no way. It had to be a mistake. Still he kept his gaze away from it as if looking at it might somehow make it coil up and strike. Hell, he'd been worried about her working too hard, when in reality he should have been worried about—

She didn't answer for several long seconds.

"Garret, I am so sorry." Her hand reached out as if she might touch him, but then changed her mind. Maybe because he hadn't made any effort to meet her halfway.

Halfway to where?

The test stick had landed upside down, but to turn it over seemed beyond his abilities. Doing so might mean the very thing he'd vowed to avoid had managed to track him down. And he wasn't sure he could hold himself together if that happened.

A million flashes of firsts shot through his skull, each more painful than the last: Leticia's birth, her first baby tooth, her first steps, her first day of school—and the last breath she ever took.

Hot daggers assaulted the backs of his eyes and he struggled to make his tongue form words.

"We used—" His voice cracked and he had to start over. "We used protection."

"I know we did." A gaze awash with compassion met his.

"Then—how?"

"I don't know. Any number of things can go wrong."

Go wrong. That was an understatement.

He finally reached for the stick and flipped it, even though he already knew what he'd find. And there it was. A pink plus sign.

Why was it that those commercials always showed everyone giddy with happiness and excitement? He had been too, at one time.

But not now. It was as if he were trapped

in a surreal world where things never quite worked out as they should. Where no one was giddy or happy.

Where there was nothing left to do but drop flowers onto a headstone. And he hadn't even been able to do that.

"You're pregnant."

"Yes."

He didn't ask if it was his. His brain might be screaming at him to find a way to escape, but his heart knew better than to listen to it.

She'd come here to—

Actually, he wasn't quite sure *why* she was there.

"What do you want me to do?"

That seemed to confuse her for a second or two. Then she stood a little straighter. "I'd like to know how you feel about it."

How he felt about it? He was pretty sure she wouldn't like his answer to that. So he rephrased and tossed the query right back to her.

"Maybe I should ask you that question, since you're suddenly putting in a lot of overtime again."

Her mouth opened. And closed, teeth coming down on her bottom lip. Then she tipped her head to one side and stared at him. "That's all you have to say? That I'm working too much overtime?"

"Can you take another test?"

"I've taken five. They're all identical. Do you want me to pull them out and show you? This is real, Garret. I have no reason to make something like this up."

"I didn't say you made it up." It had to have been from that time at her house, because they had only been at his house a couple of days ago, not long enough to register on a test.

"Did you know this was a possibility when you came to the auction? When you let me take you home afterward?"

She averted her eyes, and he knew. Before she even spoke the words. "Yes. I knew."

She sank into the chair he'd offered her moments earlier.

"And you said nothing." He swallowed. "That whole time."

Maybe she had. She'd whispered something in her sleep at his house. Something he hadn't caught, but she'd seemed distressed, stirring until he pulled her back against him.

Hell, how had this even happened? He'd

lost one child already. Wasn't that enough for one lifetime? Surely she didn't expect him to take on another one. He couldn't. He even remembered saying that to her, sometime after that first night they'd spent together.

And still she was here. Wanting some kind of answer. One he didn't think he could give her.

His gaze went to her midsection and then slid back up to her face.

Just two days ago, he'd been envisioning spending more time with her. Had even started thinking about the future.

But now that future would include a crying infant, a toddler's tendency to get into everything in sight—and the worst thing of all: a small human who would capture his heart.

And he'd worry—every second—about the millions of things that could go wrong. Just like Addy's comment about that condom.

Any number of things can go wrong.

His stomach churned up bile that frothed and burned inside him.

She slid a hand on his desk, her palm up. "You're right. I suspected I might be pregnant and didn't say anything. I should have, and I'm sorry. I didn't want to face the possibility."

Any number of things can go wrong.

Those damned words wouldn't stop pounding in his head. They just kept looping around over and over and over, reminding him of the reasons he didn't want to father another child.

"I can't do this, Addy. Any of it."

She sat there for a second and stared at him as if waiting for him to say something else. Anything else. But he was completely blank. Completely empty. Except for that single drumming phrase that wouldn't let up.

She withdrew her hand and let it fall into her lap. Up went her chin. "Then don't. Don't do this. Don't do anything."

With that, she got to her feet, drew her lanyard over her head and dropped it on his desk.

Something about that registered in the back of his head, but he couldn't quite make sense of it. He couldn't make sense of anything.

"Goodbye, Garret."

He didn't move. Didn't argue with her. Just let her slowly climb to her feet and walk toward the door. And then she was through it, shutting it behind her. Only then did the words finally slow to a stop.

Any number of things can go wrong.

Garret was pretty sure something had just gone very wrong. And he had no idea how to make it right. Or if he should even try.

CHAPTER TWELVE

Damn Garret Stapleton for making her care. Why hadn't he walked away after that first kiss on the beach?

Why hadn't she?

She didn't know. What she did know was that the night of the auction, after Garret had given his last speech and had headed her way, something profound had happened inside her. Something that had nothing to do with the new life she carried.

He was charming and sexy, and had a heart as big as the whole state of Florida. Only that heart had no room in it for a child. His child. He'd said so himself.

And that hurt more than she'd believed possible.

The baby she'd never dreamed she'd have was suddenly a very real possibility. And she was already in love with him or her. If she had to raise the child to adulthood on her own, then so be it.

Except she didn't want that. She wanted the entire glorious dream, not just part of it. And that included Garret.

Oh, he'd tried to call her after she'd walked out of his office. Three times, actually, over the last two weeks.

She had finally attempted to call the hospital yesterday afternoon on the off chance that he'd changed his mind, but when she'd asked to speak with him, she'd been told he was out of town.

A shiver had gone through her. "Do you know where he went?"

"New York City. He's not sure when he'll be back."

Or if.

The operator hadn't exactly said it, but it seemed to hang in the air.

Had he actually left permanently?

The pain in her heart threatened to overwhelm her.

She'd made a huge mistake by not telling him at the auction that her period was late. But she'd told herself that it was probably all a big mistake. That the timing was just off due to stress.

Only it hadn't been stress, and when she'd dropped that test stick on his desk, she might as well have dropped an anvil on his head. Maybe she had. She just hadn't been able to think of a better way to present it. All options seemed to lead to the same disastrous end.

And now he might be gone forever.

She'd quit *her* job over it, hadn't she? Was it so surprising that he might choose to do the same?

No, it wasn't. She could imagine him wanting to get as far away from the problem as possible. Just as her hurt and anger had driven her to walk out of his office.

Except Addy didn't see the baby as a problem. Not anymore. She'd come to see it as a blessing.

The fact that Garret didn't view the situation through the same lens had nothing to do with her.

She'd just have to learn to live with it. Somehow.

Until then, she could try taking the advice she'd given Garret all those weeks ago.

She could try doing a little surf therapy. And hope that it really could work miracles.

Garret stood over his daughter's grave, unsure and alone. He could turn and walk away, and go back to life the way it was. Life before Addy's revelation. Or he could make a change. Turn a corner.

Except he couldn't see what lay around that corner. And that was where the fear came from. If he could see the future, it would make his decision a whole lot easier.

Only he wasn't a prophet. And neither was Addy.

What if she decided she couldn't raise a child on her own and did something about it?

His gut twisted. Was that what he wanted?

No. It wasn't. But was that really fair to her? He didn't want any part of what she'd told him, but he expected her to figure it out and make the best of it. While he turned a blind eye to everything and pretended it didn't exist.

Only it did.

He knelt beside the granite marker, laying what he'd brought to the side. He then touched the name engraved in the stone with the tip of his finger.

"Sorry I haven't been here in a while, sweetheart."

A while? That was an understatement.

He dusted a blade of grass off the stone. He'd needed to come here. Had needed to think.

He picked up his offering and laid it in front of the headstone. Daisies. Leticia's favorite flower.

And his too.

"I'm not sure what I should do. Or if I should do anything."

His head had been filled with nothing but Addy for the last two weeks. With the terrible sadness he'd seen in her expression when she took off her lanyard and placed it on his desk. He hadn't realized the significance of that act at first. He'd been too hung up on that pink symbol on the pregnancy test to care about anything else. Until the door had closed and he'd realized she'd just quit.

He'd quickly stuck the test strip in his desk and done his best to forget about it.

Only he hadn't been able to. Every time he'd opened that drawer, it had stared up at him in accusation. She'd trusted him enough to tell him she was pregnant, and he'd thrown it back in her face. And now as he sat in the spot where his life had changed forever, he wondered if he'd been the biggest fool on the planet.

Oh, he had been. Of that there was no doubt.

"Oh, Letty. You wouldn't be very happy with me right now."

He glanced at his ruined hand, lips twisting at what he'd done to himself all those years ago. What he was doing to himself all over again. What he was doing to Addy.

Addy.

He stared at the stone, a thought coming to him. He'd just thought about making a change and turning a corner. Except the fear of what might lie around that corner was keeping him from moving forward.

He forced himself to stop and look at the corner, to envision what might be waiting for him around that bend in the road.

Oh, hell. He swallowed as a realization pushed up from somewhere deep inside him.

It was Addy. She was what was around the

corner. She and that tiny creature she carried inside her.

Wasn't knowing that enough? Did other people gain any more insight into their future than what he'd been given?

He didn't think so.

If he chose not to turn that corner, one thing was certain. He was going to lose her forever. Lose a chance at happiness. Was he willing to pay that kind of price to protect himself from pain? Wouldn't doing that just cause a completely different kind of pain?

He loved her. With all his heart. On some level he'd realized that back at the hospital and had tried to call her, even though he hadn't been sure what he was going to say. But she'd evidently not been ready to talk to him. Maybe she'd never be ready.

He'd never know if he didn't try.

But first, he needed to finally close the door on his past. A past he couldn't change, but one he could hopefully learn from.

"I think I know what I need to do." He scooted the daisies closer to the stone. "If things work out the way I hope they will, I might not be back for a while, but you'll have flowers on every birthday. I promise."

He kissed his fingers and touched them to her name. "You're going to be a big sister. God, I hope I do you proud as her father."

A rush of moisture blurred the writing. "Until next time, baby. I love you."

With that, he stood, praying that somehow Addy was still waiting. Just around that corner.

He sat on the beach for the third day in a row, his board beside him. He had no idea if she would even come, but he could hope. The hospital said she'd called once while he was in New York, but that she hadn't tried again.

He'd left her a voice mail on his way back from the airport asking her to meet him at their spot. He could only hope it wasn't too late.

If she didn't show up soon, he wasn't sure what he was going to do. Her house was empty, a For Sale sign planted in the yard.

That worried him.

The sun was hot and a trickle of sweat ran down his temple. He lifted his forearm to swipe it away. She evidently wasn't coming today either.

Just as he started to get up, he spied a familiar movement off in the distance. A flash of red. A gentle sway of hips. A surfboard held to her side.

A dream?

The vision kept coming, and he swallowed when he realized she was very real. She wore the same red bikini she'd worn the first time they came here.

She stopped in front of him and dropped her board, fin-side up, on the sand. "You're dry. You haven't been in yet?" There was no smile on her face. No clue as to what she was thinking.

"I was getting ready to leave, actually."

A frown formed. "I thought you asked me to meet you here at three."

"That was two days ago."

"And you're still here?"

A ghost of a grin found its way to his mouth. "Maybe I should have camped out." The smile disappeared. "I thought you weren't coming."

"I was in court finalizing my divorce when your call came in."

"And yesterday?"

"Doctor's appointment. Right at three." The words had a wary sound to them.

What kind of appointment? A trickle of fear slid across his heart. "Is everything—?"

"Yes. Still pregnant. Sorry."

Reaching up, he gripped her hand. "I'm glad." He patted his towel. "Can you sit down? I have a few things I want to say, starting with I'm sorry."

There was a momentary hesitation and then she eased down beside him.

"Sorry?"

"Yes. For all of it." He gazed out toward the sea. "I was shocked. And frankly terrified. I never expected to become a father again."

"I know. I was pretty shocked and terrified too at the way things happened. Only I can't run away from the reality of what's happening inside of me, like you can. Like you *did*." She stared at the sand. "You hurt me."

"I know. And I'm sorry. I went to visit Leticia's grave."

She looked up. "That's why you went to New York?"

"Yes. I needed to make peace with my past, and wanted time to work through some things about myself." He took her hand again, grateful when she didn't jerk away from him.

"I also took her some flowers. Someone I care about very much made me realize how important that is."

"Oh, Garret." Moisture appeared in her eyes. "I'm so glad."

He threaded his fingers through hers. "I told her she's going to be a big sister. And that I would bring him or her to visit."

She didn't say anything for several long seconds and a different kind of agony went through him. Then her fingers tightened around his, squeezing as if she needed something to hang on to.

"Does this mean that you want to be a part of the baby's life?"

"I want more than that, Addy. I want to be a part of your life. If you'll let me." He lifted her hand and kissed it. "I love you. More than you can know. Can you forgive me for taking off like I did when you told me?"

"But you didn't. You sat right there in your office and barely moved. Barely looked at me."

"It may have seemed that way, but inside my head, I was running. The second I said 'I can't do this,' I was out of there." He covered their joined hands with his damaged one. "And now I'm done running."

She shifted her body toward him. "You need to be sure. Very sure. I don't want someone who will be there for a while and then start drifting away when things get hard. Or a crisis happens. I've done that once. I won't settle for it a second time. And I don't want that for our child."

"I'm very sure. I want to spend the rest of my life with you. I'm even thinking of weaning away from some of my administrative duties and moving back toward medicine itself."

"You are?" There was no mistaking the shock on her face.

"I've been researching diagnosticians in the field of neurology. It's actually a thing."

"That's wonderful."

"You're the one who made me think it was possible." A thought came to him. "Your house is up for sale."

"Yes. I've made peace with my past too. And I'm getting rid of the parts that no longer fit."

His heart chilled. Was he one of those parts? "I need to know how you feel about me."

"Isn't it obvious?"

"Maybe to you, but not to me."

She let go of his good hand, fingers curling around his damaged one. She held it tight. "I love you, Garret Stapleton. I think I have since that first day on the beach—when you tried the pop up, even though it hurt this hand so badly. And you kept on trying. You didn't give up. After I realized I was pregnant, I hoped and prayed that you wouldn't give up on me either. On us."

"Never." A stream of pure hope rushed over him, peeling away the fear and doubt. "And then there were three."

She smiled. "Unless there are four."

"Four?"

Before the panicked thought could fully take root, she shook her head. "I'm kidding. I just wanted to make sure you were serious about the not running part."

"I am not going anywhere."

"Even though this has all happened as quickly as it has?"

He smiled. "Well, you took the quick route with your last marriage and I took the slow route, and neither of those worked. Maybe it wasn't a matter of timing. Maybe it was a matter of finding the right person at the right time."

"That means you're willing to give us a try? All of us?" She slid closer, linking her arm with his.

"You coaxed me into the water. And onto a surfboard. I think after those two things, this 'rest of our lives' gig might just be a piece of cake."

She tilted her head to look at him. "Garret, I think, just this once, you might be right."

EPILOGUE

THIS LIFE WAS a piece of cake. Literally.

She blew out the single white candle and made a wish. Except all her wishes had already come true. So she had to settle for a silly one about her baby taking after his handsome daddy. The sonogram had revealed their child was going to be a boy.

And he was all alone in there, much to Garret's disappointment. He had whispered late one night as he'd held her that maybe they should have a second one. She was fine with that, but she would really rather they had them one at a time.

He came up behind her and curved his hands around her midsection. Eight months along and she felt huge and unwieldy, but Garret made her feel beautiful, even when her feet swelled and she had to fan herself against the South Beach heat and humidity.

"I have a present for you."

She leaned her head against his chest, reveling in the fact that this man was hers and hers alone. "You smell good."

He chuckled. "That doesn't track with what I just said. At all."

"It tracks in my head—that's all that matters."

He kissed her temple, then took her by the hand. "Come on. I've been keeping this a secret for far too long, and, let me tell you, it hasn't been easy."

"A secret?"

"Yep."

He led her to the spare bedroom that would soon be the baby's nursery. Garret had been in there for a long time yesterday painting and getting things ready.

Or so he'd said.

Addy was happier than she'd believed possible.

"What is it?"

"Open the door and see."

Giving him a puzzled glance, she turned the knob and pushed on the door. At first all she saw were the same furnishings and ocean motifs that Garret had worked so hard on. Then, against the wall, she spied a large curved board. A surfboard.

No. Not just a surfboard—a *long*board.

Her breath caught in her lungs. "I know this board."

Making her way toward it, she ran her fingers down the warm glossy wood and closed her eyes, trying to remember where…

It came to her in a flash.

"The auction. This is the board from the beach cabana."

"I hoped you'd recognize it."

"I remember wanting that board." She turned toward him. "But how? I was there when the bidding was going on. I saw the man with the paddle."

"He's a hospital employee. I asked him to bid on it for me."

"You bought this for me? All the way back then?"

He stood in front of her and cupped her face in his hands. "I knew I loved you all the way back then. I just had to grow into it."

"Grow into it. I like that." There was no hint of Garret giving up or backing out. He'd told the truth. He was done running. And so was she.

She looked wistfully at the board and gave a huge sigh. "I wish I could use it, but I'd have to do a backstroke to get it to go anywhere. And I'm afraid my pop up might turn into a pop *out*. And I don't think South Beach is quite ready to see me give birth on the beach."

"I know of a doctor who would be nearby to assist."

Garret was still the hospital administrator. For now. But he'd kept his promise to himself. He was doing some consulting on the side, and, a year from now, he was going to be employed by the hospital as its very first neurological diagnostician, working with a team of other neurologists.

She was ecstatic, even as Garret remained cautiously optimistic. But she loved that about him.

"I happen to know that doctor. And he's excellent at a lot of things. But I would rather have this baby in the comfort of the hospital. *Our* hospital."

She twined her arms around her husband's neck and lifted her face for a kiss. It lingered, and then deepened until Garret finally pulled away with a shaky laugh. "I do not want to be the cause of that baby coming before he's ready."

Arching, she pressed her hands against the small of her back. "But what if I'm ready?"

He gently turned her so that she was facing away from him and massaged the area he knew bothered her, his right hand cupping her hip and using his thumb to apply pressure to her sore muscles.

"Mmm…that feels so good."

"Come to bed, Addy, where I can make you feel even better." The murmured words were said in that sexy baritone that made her knees knock. He wasn't talking about sex. Or even about making out. He really did just want to make her feel better, and if that wasn't love, she didn't know what was.

"Cake first?"

"Of course. What was I thinking?"

Giving the board one last look, she linked arms with her husband and closed the door, heading into a future that promised to be filled with plenty of surf therapy, a little bit of cake and a whole lot of love.

* * * * *

*If you enjoyed this story, check out
these other great reads from
Tina Beckett*

The Billionaire's Christmas Wish
Tempted by Dr. Patera
The Doctors' Baby Miracle
From Passion to Pregnancy

All available now!